THE
LIGHT BEYOND
THE FOREST

The Quest for the Holy Grail

Rosemary Sutcliff

Decorations by
SHIRLEY FELTS

PUFFIN BOOKS

PUFFIN BOOKS

Published by the Penguin Group

Penguin Books USA Inc., 375 Hudson Street, New York, New York 10014, U.S.A.

Penguin Books Ltd, 27 Wrights Lane, London W8 5TZ, England

Penguin Books Australia Ltd, Ringwood, Victoria, Australia

Penguin Books Canada Ltd, 10 Alcorn Avenue, Toronto, Ontario, Canada M4V 3B2

Penguin Books (N.Z.) Ltd, 182-190 Wairau Road, Auckland 10, New Zealand

Penguin Books Ltd, Registered Offices: Harmondsworth, Middlesex, England

First published in Great Britain by the Bodley Head, 1979
First published in the United States of America by E. P. Dutton,
a division of Elsevier-Dutton Publishing Company, Inc., 1980
Published in Puffin Books, 1994

20 19 18 17 16 15 14 13 12 11

THE LIBRARY OF CONGRESS HAS CATALOGED THE E. P. DUTTON EDITION AS FOLLOWS:
Sutcliff, Rosemary.
The light beyond the forest.
Summary: A retelling of the adventures of King Arthur's knights,
Sir Lancelot, Sir Galahad, Sir Bors, and Sir Percival,
as they search for the Holy Grail.
1. Arthurian romance. [1. Grail. 2. Knights and knighthood. 3. Arthur, King] I. Felts, Shirley. II. Title.
PZ8.1.S95Li   1980   398.2'6   79-23396   0-525-33665-6

Puffin Books ISBN 0-14-037150-8

Printed in the United States of America

CONTENTS

AUTHOR'S NOTE

The story of how the Knights of the Round Table went questing for the Holy Grail, as we have known it for the past eight hundred years or so, and as Sir Thomas Malory retold it so superbly in *Morte d'Arthur*, stands out on its own from among all the rest of the Arthurian legends, because above them all, it is a Christian story and carries within it the things of the Spirit that seemed especially important to the people of the Middle Ages. At one level it is the story of King Arthur's knights searching for the cup of the Last Supper; on a deeper level, like *The Pilgrim's Progress*, it is an account of Man's search for God. But the medieval Christian story is shot through with shadows and half-light and haunting echoes of much older things; scraps of the mystery religions which the legions carried from end to end of the Roman Empire; above all, a mass of Celtic myth and folklore. For, despite its medieval French and German and English tellings and re-tellings, the Grail Quest, like all the other Arthurian legends, is Celtic in its beginnings. The Celts also had their quest stories, their unexplained happenings and shifting forests and beckoning lights. They had their cup (only for them it was a cauldron) and spear and sword and stone, which were the four treasures of Anwn, that strange realm which was both the World of the Dead and the World of Faery.

In reading *The Light Beyond the Forest* try to remember, as I have done all the time I was writing it, the shadows and the half-lights and the echoes behind.

Two things I think I should explain. One is that in medieval times dinner was at about ten o'clock in the morning and supper at about six in the evening. The other is that a tilt or joust was a trial of strength and skill between two knights at a time; a form of sport, though a dangerous one; but a tournament was a kind of sham battle between any number, which frequently got out of hand and ended in a lot of people being killed.

THE NEW-MADE KNIGHT

On every side, Camelot climbed, roof above coloured roof, up the steep slopes of the hill. About the foot of the hill the river cast its shining silver noose; and at the highest heart of the town rose the palace of King Arthur. And in the Great Hall of Arthur's palace stood the Round Table, which could seat a hundred and fifty knights, each with his name written in fairest gold on the high back of his chair behind him: the Knights of the Fellowship of the Round Table, which had been formed long ago when Arthur was new and young to his kingship, for the spreading of justice and mercy and chivalry and the upholding of right against might throughout the land.

Wherever the knights might be at other times—for they had lives of their own to lead, and quests of their own to follow—it was their custom always to gather to the King for the great feast days of the Church. And so one Pentecost Eve they were assembled and just sitting down to supper, when a maiden came riding into the hall on a horse all lathered with sweat from the speed that she had made.

And she called upon Sir Lancelot of the Lake, who was the greatest of all the Round Table knights, to ride with her, in the name of King Pelles, whom she served.

"What thing is it that King Pelles wants of me?" asked Sir Lancelot.

"That you shall know in good time."

Sir Lancelot sat looking at his big bony sword hand on the table, while the past stirred within him, and his heart twisted a little with old sorrows and new foreshadowings. Then he rose from his place, all his companions looking on, and called for a squire to saddle his horse and another to bring his armour.

And he rode with the maiden as she asked, down from the palace and across the three-spanned bridge, and into the green young-summer mazes of the forest.

Soon he found that they were following a path that he had never followed before in all the years that he had known those forest ways; and after a league or less it brought them out into a broad clearing that was strange to him also; where the grey buildings of a nunnery sat peacefully among orchards and herb gardens beside the way. As they drew near, the gates were opened as if those within had been watching for them; and convent servants came to take Sir Lancelot's horse, while others led him to a fair and high-ceilinged guest chamber.

There was a bed in the middle of the chamber, and on it two knights lay asleep, and looking at their russet-brown heads burrowed into the pillows, Sir Lancelot saw that they were two young kinsmen of his, Bors and Lional, who he supposed must be on their way to the Round Table gathering. He laughed, and shook each by the shoulder to rouse them, and they plunged awake, reaching for their daggers before they saw who it was.

And while they were still exclaiming and greeting each other, the abbess and two of her nuns came into the chamber, bringing with them a very young man. At their coming, the laughing and the horseplay ceased; and a great quiet came with them into the chamber.

"Sir Lancelot," said the abbess, "we bring you this boy whom we have raised up and loved as our own, ever since his mother died, before he stood as tall as a sword-blade from the ground. Now it is time that he becomes a knight, and his grandsire, King Pelles, would have him receive his knighthood from your hand."

And the quiet closed in again after her words; and in the midst of it Sir Lancelot and the boy stood and looked at each other.

Now Sir Lancelot of the Lake was an ugly man, with an ugliness such as women love. His dark face under the thick badger-streaked hair looked as though it had been put together in haste, so that the two sides of it did not match. One side of his mouth was grave with heavy thought, while the other lifted in joy; one eyebrow was level as a falcon's wing and the other flew wild like a mongrel's ear. He had lived forty-five summers and winters in the world, and loved and sorrowed and triumphed and fought to the utmost, and every joy and sorrow and striving had set its mark on him.

The boy's face was pale and clear, waiting for life to touch it, and his hair made a smooth cap as of dark silk on his head. He was like his mother, Elaine, the daughter of King Pelles; and Sir Lancelot saw that in the first moment that they turned to each other. But the look which had made men call Elaine 'The Lily' in him made them think of a spear-blade or a still tall flame.

Yet from the strong chaos of Sir Lancelot's face, and the waiting quietness of the boy's, the same wide grey eyes looked long and steady out at each other.

And Sir Bors and Sir Lional, watching, exchanged quick startled glances.

"What is your name?" said Sir Lancelot, at last.

"Galahad," said the boy.

There was a sudden wild weeping deep down in Lancelot where no one but he could know of it. All the years of his manhood he had loved Guenever, King Arthur's queen, and for her sake had never looked towards another woman. But there had been a time, long ago, when King Pelles' daughter had set her love on him and, being desperate, had won him to her by a trick for just one night. And of that one night she had borne a son, and called him Galahad.

"My name also was Galahad, before I gained my second name that now men call me by," said Lancelot. And then knew that he need not have said it, for his son already knew.

To the lady abbess he said, "Madam, let him keep his vigil in the church tonight, and it shall be as his grandsire wishes in the morning."

So that night Galahad kept his vigil, kneeling before the high altar of the nunnery church; and when the birds woke to their singing in the first light of Pentecost morning, Sir Lancelot dubbed him knight.

"Now come with us to King Arthur's court," he said, when it was done.

But the abbess shook her head. "Not yet. Go you back to Camelot; and when it is the right time, he will come."

So Sir Lancelot and his young cousins rode back to Camelot alone. And all the way Sir Lancelot looked straight between his horse's ears and spoke not one word.

When they reached Camelot, the King and Queen had gone with all their court to hear morning Mass, and it was too late to join them. So the three knights went into the Great Hall to wait for their return. And there they found a most strange thing.

This was the way of it.

Long before, when the Fellowship was formed, Merlin the old and wise, the master of secret knowledge, who had taught Arthur those things which a king should know, had made for him by magic arts the Round Table with its places for a hundred and fifty knights. But no more than a hundred and forty-nine had ever sat down at that table, while always the last seat remained empty. And this seat was called the Seat Perilous, for no man might sit in it that disaster did not befall him. Now Merlin, who had forgotten his wisdom and given his heart to an enchantress because she smiled at him and was beautiful, slept where she had locked him in a magic hawthorn tree; and for twenty years and more, Arthur and his brotherhood had sat at his Round Table with the empty seat among them. And some of those who had sat there in the early years were dead now, and new young knights come to fill their places; and others were scarred by old battles and had grey in their hair that had been black or gold or brown when first they gathered there. And still the Seat Perilous remained empty and waiting.

But now the sun falling through one of the high windows touched the carved and beautiful chair, and on its high back something glinted in the light. And drawing near, the three knights read, in letters that seemed that moment to have been set there in new-fired gold: "Four hundred and fifty years have passed since the Passion of Our Lord Jesus Christ. And on the day of Pentecost this seat shall find its master."

"That is today," said Sir Lancelot, at half breath.

And Sir Bors, scarce knowing why he did so—and he was not one to do things without clear reason—spread his cloak over the back of the Seat Perilous, so that the words were hidden until their moment came.

In due time the King and Queen and all the court returned from Mass, and greeted the newcomers; and the King asked Sir Lancelot how his venture of the day before had gone. Sir Lancelot told how the maiden had taken him to a nunnery, and how there he had knighted a young man who was King Pelles' grandson. But he said no more as to the boy, for he thought, "Every one will know, soon enough." Yet the Queen must have guessed, for she bade them all God's greeting and withdrew quickly to her own chambers, her ladies going with her.

Then the pages began to set the table for dinner; but just as the knights were about to take their places, a squire came running, crying out as he burst upon them, "Sirs—my Lord King—there is a great wonder—"

"And what wonder is that?" said the King. He was hungry.

"A stone—a great stone floating as light as a leaf along the river; and in the stone a sword standing upright! With my own eyes I saw it!"

The King remembered another sword in another stone, and how he had pulled it out and so proved himself the true fore-chosen King of Britain; and he forgot his hunger. And with all his knights behind him he went down from the palace to the river bank. There, caught by an out-thrust of rooty bank, they found a block of red marble, and standing upright in it a sword with a pommel formed of a ball of amber as large as an apple. And engraved on the quillions in letters of gold they read: "None shall take me hence, but he at whose side I am to hang. And he shall be the best knight in the world."

Arthur knew that his own sword and its stone were past and behind him; and he called to Sir Lancelot who was nearest and dearest to him of all his knights, "This sword all but has your name on it."

"Not mine, my lord the King." Lancelot did not know why he said it. It was not modesty. He knew his own reputation as well as the world knew it. But he knew that it had to be said.

"Try," said the King.

"No," said Lancelot, and his hand went to the hilt of the sword at his side. "I have Joyeux; why should I turn faithlessly to seek another blade?" And his mouth shut like a trap and he moved no nearer.

Then at the King's bidding Sir Gawain of Orkney, who was the King's nephew and loved him well, set his two hands to the sword-grip and pulled until the veins stood out on his neck, but could not shift the blade; and then young Sir Percival of Wales spat on his hands and tried, more to keep Sir Gawain company than anything else, for he was a large, kind, simple-hearted young man and had no high opinion of himself. After he, too, had failed, no one else came forward; and so after a while they left the sword in its block of red marble among the alder roots, and went back to the Great Hall to dinner.

But another marvel was to come upon them before they ate that day.

For when they were all seated, and with a ringing and singing and sounding of horns the first dishes had just been borne in, suddenly, and without any hand touching them, all the doors and window-shutters slammed to as in a squall of wind. Yet there was no wind. And the Hall was still lit as though with the clear brightness of the day outside.

All round the table men looked at each other with startled faces. And in the same instant, none seeing how they came, there were two strangers among them; an old man robed in white, and beside him a knight whose surcoat over his armour blazed red as though he were a tongue of flame, but with no shield over his shoulder and only an empty sheath hanging from his sword belt.

"Peace be with you," said the old man to the King.

"And with you, stranger," returned the King. But his gaze went to the knight in the scarlet surcoat.

"Sir," said the old man, "I bring before you this knight of the line of King Pelles, and through him of the line of Joseph of Arimathea; he who brought to this land the Holy Grail, from the land where Our Lord Jesus Christ drank from that wondrous cup, and shared its wine with his disciples when they gathered to the Last Supper. That was the beginning of the mystery of the Grail's sojourn among men; and many wonders and many sorrows have followed therefrom; and because of it King Pelles himself lies maimed of a wound that never heals and his land is a wilderness; but now the time comes for the ending of all these things. And with the time, comes the knight who shall bring them to fulfilment and surcease."

"If it be as you say," said the King, "there was no man ever more welcome."

Then the old man, serving the knight as though he were his squire, helped him to disarm and put his flame-red surcoat on again over his white tunic. And now that his head was bared, many were the eyes that went from his face to Sir Lancelot's and back again. And the old man led him straight to the Seat Perilous, and pulled aside Bors's cloak, so that the golden lettering shone out once more. But the words had changed since Bors had covered them, and now they read: "This is the seat of Galahad."

The young knight sat down in it, very grave and still. He looked at the old man and said, "Faithfully you have done what was demanded of you. Now go back to Corbenic as you came. Greet my grandsire, and tell him that I will surely come when the time brings me."

And the ancient man went to the great door, and opened it, no one daring to move or follow him, and went his way.

Behind him, the King and all his knights set themselves to making Sir Galahad welcome. They would have done the same for any newcomer to their brotherhood. But from the old man's words, they had added reason for gladness at his coming. They knew well enough, all of them, of King Pelles, who men called the Grail Keeper, the Fisher King, and who they called also the Maimed King because of the wound he had in his thigh that never healed; and they knew that because of this wound, his land suffered also, bound by drought and lean harvests and the shadow of sorrows and strange happenings that hung over it like a cloud. Now, it seemed, through the new young knight in their midst, all this was to be mended; and so they rejoiced.

But for another reason also they were glad. For a long while they had felt, the older knights especially, that in Camelot the high and shining days were over, that the long struggle for right against might was behind them, and the dreams were done with, and life had settled into a solid mould; and there was a weariness of heart among the Fellowship of the Round Table. Now there was something ahead of them again, instead of all in the past. Something coming; joy or grief, maybe death, but something coming . . .

"A light beyond the forest," thought Sir Lancelot, "but the dark forest to be traversed first." And was not quite sure why he had thought it.

"If I were a tree, and spring was coming—a long way off, but still coming—this is how I should feel," thought Sir Percival, and his wide serious gaze was on the young knight who sat so gravely and calmly in the forbidden seat. Sir Percival was a born follower, and to such a one there is nothing better in the world than to find the leader his heart goes out to.

"How is it that he can sit there, and no harm come to him?" said Sir Bors, worried, to Sir Lancelot beside him. "He has had no time yet to prove his worthiness."

And Sir Lancelot said, "Did you not see his name on the back? I am thinking it could only be because God would have him sitting there."

2

THE THUNDER
AND THE SUNBEAM

As the meal drew to its end, the King was telling his newest knight of the wonder that they had all seen that morning before his coming. "Since the seat is for you, it may be that the sword is for you also," said the King. "Come, and we will put the matter to the test."

So again the knights went down through the steep narrow streets of Camelot, where the swallows darted between the eaves in the summer air; and again they gathered on the river bank.

The block of red marble still lay stranded among the alder roots, and the strange and beautiful sword still stood fast in it.

And Sir Galahad stepped down among the wet roots where the water ran shallow under the bank, and drew the sword from its stone as sweetly as from a well-oiled sheath.

A gasp broke from the watching knights; and the King said, "Surely here is a wonder indeed! Two of my best knights have failed in that attempt."

Sir Galahad stood looking at the sword in his hand, feeling its balance. "The adventure was not theirs, but mine," he said, not boasting but simply stating the simple fact, and slid the blade into the empty sheath at his side. "I am no longer a knight without a sword. All that I need now is a shield."

"God shall send you a shield, even as he has sent you the sword," said the King.

And Sir Lancelot remembered the words on the hilt, and beat down a bitter sense of loss, telling himself that no man could be for ever the best knight in the world, able to tell himself that, because he did not yet quite believe it.

Then the King spoke again, "My brothers, the thought is on me that soon we are to scatter, and never again shall I see you all here with me as you are now. Therefore, for the rest of this day, let us hold a joust here in the meadows below Camelot, and do such deeds that after our time is past, old men shall tell of it to their grandsons by the fire on winter nights, and the children's eyes shall shine at the hearing, and they shall tell of it to their grandsons in turn."

So the lists were set up, and men sent for their horses

and weapons, and all the rest of that day while the sunlight lasted the knights jousted on the level ground below Camelot. And men looked to see how Sir Galahad would show, seeing that he had had so strange an upbringing and had maybe never learned to carry arms. But he proved himself so well, both as a horse-master and with sword and lance, that by sunset, of all those who had come against him, Sir Lancelot and Sir Percival were the only two he had not been able to unhorse.

And when the dusk thickened over the river meadows, they made an end, and rode back up the streets of Camelot town, with all the townsfolk who had come down to watch straggling home again behind them. And so they went back into the palace, for it was time for the evening meal.

But the wonders of that day were not yet over.

When the knights had unarmed and sat themselves once more at table, when the torches had been lit and the linen board-cloths were spread, there came a clap of thunder so loud that it seemed the very roof must fall. And after the thunder there came a sunbeam that struck like a sword through the Hall, dimming out the torches and lighting every corner to seven times the radiance of broad day. And it seemed to all those about the table that the light shone into their very souls; and a great awe fell upon them; a great stillness so that they could neither move nor speak.

And as they sat so, the Holy Grail came in to the Hall, no man seeing the hands that carried it.

It entered through the great door, veiled with a cloth of fine white samite as every man there had seen the Communion Cup veiled upon the altar at the celebration of the Mass. And so the knowledge came into their hearts of what it was they looked upon. It seemed to float of itself, light and still as a sunbeam upon the air; and at its coming the high Hall was flooded with a thousand fragrances, as though all the flowers and spices of the world had been poured out before it. Slowly, it circled the vast table, hovering before each man, and passing on; and each man, after it had passed him by, found spread before him food far more delicious than any that ever came out of the palace kitchens.

And when it had circled the table, as silently as it had come, the Grail passed from their sight.

The sunbeam faded and the torches brightened again in the smoky shadows, and the stillness passed from the men sitting there. And the King said, but still quietly, "My brothers, now our hearts should be lifted up for joy, that Our Lord has shown so great a sign of his love, in feeding us with his grace from his own cup at this high feast of Pentecost. Now indeed we know that the time is come of which the old man spoke, who brought Sir Galahad among us."

And Sir Gawain, who was ever among the quickest to take fire of all the Round Table brotherhood, sprang to his feet and swore that next morning he would ride out upon the Quest of the Holy Grail, and never return to court until he had looked openly upon the mystery which that day they had been allowed to glimpse; and until the freeing of King Pelles' Waste Land had been brought about, as the old man had foretold.

And on hearing him, every knight in the Hall sprang up and took upon himself the same oath.

But the King bent his face into his hands, and the tears ran between his fingers. "Gawain, Gawain, you fill my heart with grief. For now indeed I know that we are to scatter; and I must lose the best and truest companions that ever a man had. And well I know that many of you, the flower of those who ride away, will not return to me again."

And yet he knew that if it were not Gawain, then another must have done the thing, for it was fore-ordained.

"Sir," said Sir Lancelot, striving to comfort him, "if every one of us is to meet death upon this quest, we could meet it in no sweeter nor more honourable way."

But the King was not comforted.

Now word of Galahad's coming, and of his taking the sword from its stone, had reached the Queen's apartments, and she had gone out with her ladies to watch the jousting from the rampart-walk. Guessing who the new young knight must be, she longed to see him, but dared not see him too close, for she knew that the seeing would be like a dagger in her heart. And back in her own apartments at supper she had heard the thunder, and one of the squires had brought her word of the coming of the Grail, and the oath that Sir Gawain and all the knights after him had sworn.

"Sir Lancelot, too?" she said, and drove the needle through the lily that she was embroidering, deep into her finger.

"He would not be Sir Lancelot else!" said the boy.

And the red blood sprang out and made a crimson fleck on the lily petal.

Next morning when the knights were arming and their horses being walked up and down in the great courtyard, the Queen bathed her eyes that no one might know she had passed the night in weeping, and went out to bid them God speed. But at the last, her courage broke in her hand, and she turned back into the castle garden, to hide her grief, and flung herself down full-length on a low turf-seat under a pleached vine arbour.

Sir Lancelot, standing harnessed and ready to mount, saw her face in the moment that she turned away, and left his horse to the nearest squire, and went quickly and quietly after her.

The King was not looking that way. Sometimes he found it hard not to know how it was between his wife and his best friend. But so long as he did not know, he had no need to hurt the two people dearest to him on earth. He prayed, so deep down within him that he was not even aware of it, that notning would ever happen that would force him to know.

And Sir Lancelot went through the narrow door into the garden.

He stood over Guenever, and touched her silken sleeve, and she cried out to him, "You have betrayed me and given me up to death!"

"Would you have had me hang back, when the others swore to take up the Quest?"

"Yes! Rather than quit the service of my lord the King to go to strange lands from which only God can bring you safely back!"

"If it is his will," said Lancelot, "then God will bring me safely back."

"I am sick with dread!" cried the Queen, not listening. "If you loved me truly, you could not go without my leave!"

"Madam," said Sir Lancelot, "the horses are stamping in the courtyard. Give me your leave to go now."

She was silent a moment, and then she said, "I have seen Galahad, as he rode up from the jousting. He is very like you."

"He is beautiful," said Lancelot.

"So are you—so are you!" and she broke into weeping laughter, and turned and took his strange face between her hands. "I grieve for his mother, for though she bore your son, I have had more joy of you than ever she had!"

"Lady," said Lancelot, and his voice cracked in his throat, "give me leave to go."

"Go," she said, "and God be with you."

And Lancelot went back to the courtyard where all the rest were mounted and ready to be off. There with the rest, he took his leave of Arthur, his liege lord and his dearest friend; and that, too, was sharp pain within him, the more so for that he was torn with guilt because of the Queen.

"God be with you," said the King.

And they mounted and rode away, Sir Percival as close as might be behind Sir Galahad.

And all Camelot wept to see them go.

Sir Galahad, who had been born in the Castle of Corbenic, and bred there through his first years, and whose grandsire was King Pelles, knew well enough where the Grail was lodged. Sir Lancelot knew it too. But they knew also, as did every knight setting out from Arthur's court that morning, that simply to ride to Corbenic and beat upon the castle gate, demanding to see the mystery within, would serve but an empty purpose. They must cast themselves on fate, welcoming whichever way it took them, and trusting that when the time was right, if they proved worthy, the quest they followed would bring them to the place of their hearts' desire and the thing that their spirits reached out to.

So they parted from each other when they had crossed the river, and took to the forest singly, wherever the trees were thickest and there was no path. And the forest closed over behind them as though they had never been.

3
THE SHIELD OF
KING MORDRAIN

Now the story tells that when Sir Galahad had parted from the rest, he rode four days, meeting with no adventures. But on the evening of the fifth day he came to an abbey of Cistercian monks; and there he found two more of the Companions of the Round Table: King Bagdemagus and Sir Owain the Bastard. They greeted each other joyfully, and that evening, when they had eaten with the brothers, they went out into the abbey orchard, and sat themselves down under an apple tree to talk and exchange any news of the past few days.

"This is a happy chance that brings us all three to the same place at the same time," said Sir Galahad, for courtesy's sake.

"No chance brought *us*," said King Bagdemagus, "but word of the shield."

"The shield?" said Sir Galahad.

And Sir Owain told him, "We have heard that in this abbey there is a shield, with a strong magic upon it, that any man who takes it down from its place and hangs it about his neck, unless he be worthy of it, will be slain or sore wounded within three days; and we are come to put the matter to the test."

"Tomorrow morning," said King Bagdemagus, watching a brown furred bee among the last of the tarnished apple blossom, "I shall shoulder this shield, and ride upon my fortune."

"If you fail—" began Sir Galahad, then turned to Owain the Bastard, "Pray you grant me next turn, for I have as yet no shield of my own."

So the matter was agreed between them; and next morning, when they had heard Mass, King Bagdemagus asked one of the monks where the shield of which they had heard might be.

"Are you yet another who comes seeking to bear it?" said the monk, sadly; but he took them behind the high altar of the abbey church; and there on the wall hung a great shield, white and blazoned with a cross as red as fresh-spilled blood on fresh-fallen snow.

When they had looked at it, Owain said, "Indeed, Galahad, I will yield you my turn, if our brother here fails, for surely this is a shield to be carried by the best knight in the world; and I shall not seek to take it up. I have neither the valour not the virtue to carry it. And I value my neck!"

But King Bagdemagus took it down and slipped the strap over his head and settled it on his shoulder, and strode out, calling for his horse.

A young squire belonging to the abbey saddled and brought it for him, and he mounted and rode away, followed by the squire on a sturdy cob, who was to attend him, and bring back the shield if that should be the way things went.

Galahad and Owain returned to the orchard, and sat down again under the apple tree, without a word between them. And Owain made a great business of burnishing his helmet. But Galahad sat with his hands round his updrawn knees, and gazed straight before him as though at something a very long way off.

King Bagdemagus rode some two leagues or more, until he came to a meadow sloping gently down to a willow-fringed stream. And there the adventure of the shield came upon him, for among the stream-side willows a knight in white armour sat his horse, head turned as though to look for his coming, and in the instant that he rode out from the woodshore, the waiting knight struck in his spurs and with levelled lance came thundering towards him across the open ground.

The King spurred to meet him, and they came together with a crash that rang all up and down the valley. But the combat was a short one. Bagdemagus's lance shattered on the White Knight's shield, while the point of the other's weapon took him below the shoulder, driving through the iron rings of his hauberk and on deep into the flesh, and hurled him backwards from the saddle.

Then the stranger knight dismounted, and took from the fallen King the white shield with its blood-red cross.

"That was foolish of you," said he. "For it is granted to no man to bear this shield save he that is the best knight in all Christendom." He beckoned to the squire. "Take this shield and carry it back to Sir Galahad; but having given it into his hands, bring him here again to me. Since this is the shield that he will bear henceforth, it is right that he should hear the truth concerning it."

So the squire hung the shield from his own saddle-bow, and going to King Bagdemagus where he lay, got him across his horse, and mounted behind him to hold him secure. Then, leading the cob, he rode back the way they had come.

When they reached the abbey, Galahad and Owain and the brethren saw them and came running. They lifted King Bagdemagus down from his horse and bore him to one of their guest chambers, and the Father Infirmarer brought warm water and salves and fine linen to tend to his gaping wound.

Then the squire brought the shield from where he had left it hanging at the cob's saddle-bow, and gave it to Sir Galahad. "Sir, the knight from whom King Bagdemagus got his wound sends you this, and bids you bear it from now on, for you alone have the right. Also he bids you come to him, that he may tell you all that you should know concerning it. He bids you come now, for he is waiting."

So Galahad's harness was brought, and Owain and the squire helped him to arm. And he took the great shield on his shoulder. Sir Owain would have ridden with him, but Galahad bade him remain with King Bagdemagus, and rode out alone, save for the squire to show him the way.

So they came to the meadow, and found the White

28

Knight sitting his horse among the willow trees, as still and timeless as though he and his mount were painted upon the quiet of the summer air.

And when they had greeted each other in all courtesy, Sir Galahad asked him for the story of the shield.

"Gladly I will tell it," said the knight, "for it is yours to know."

And he began the telling.

"Two and forty years after the Passion of Christ, that same Joseph of Arimathea who took his body from the cross and gave it burial, left Jerusalem, bearing with him the Holy Grail, his son and many of his people following. By God's command they set out, not knowing where; and their wanderings brought them at last to the city of Sarras, far towards the sunrise, beyond any other city of men.

"Now when they came there, they found the king of that place, Mordrain by name, at bitter war with a neighbouring king who sought to overrun his frontiers. He was set to go into battle; but Josephus the son of Joseph, who was a priest and deep-sighted beyond other men, told him that the fighting would go ill for him, for he was an infidel and could not call upon the help of God. Josephus told him of what is in the Gospels; and then he had a great white shield brought, and on its face he painted a cross, blood red; and he had a shield-cover made for it of fine white sendal. And he gave it to the King, saying, 'Carry this into battle with you, and at the point in the fighting when all seems lost, uncover it, and pray to God, the semblance of whose sacred death you bear, that you may return victorious, to receive in faith his holy law.'

"King Mordrain did as he was bidden, and at the

crown of his battle, when defeat and death seemed sure, he took the cover from his shield, praying for deliverance. And the enemy broke and crumbled before him as a sand wall where the tide sweeps in. Then he returned to Sarras with great rejoicing, and was baptized a Christian. And he remained true to that faith, and the shield ever his most honoured and beloved possession.

"The time came when, again at the bidding of God, Joseph and his son Josephus left Sarras, and brought the Grail to Britain. This you know. And here they fell into the hands of a cruel and wicked king who threw them into prison. And when at last word of this came to King Mordrain, he gathered his fighting-men and set sail for Britain, and overthrew the wicked king and set Joseph and his son and their followers free.

"So the Christian faith came to Britain; at first to Avalon of the Apple Trees, and from there spreading throughout all the land.

"And Mordrain loved Josephus so deeply that for his sake he remained in Britain and never returned to his own city. And when the time came that he must lay aside his shield, he had it lodged in the abbey where you first saw it; for it was told to him in a dream, that, after him, only the best knight in Christendom might carry it without coming to disaster, for the power there is in it."

And when he had finished the story, suddenly the White Knight was no longer there.

When they had come back to themselves from the daze in which he left them, the boy from the abbey knelt down before Sir Galahad, and begged to ride with him as his squire, the squire of the best knight in all Christendom.

But Galahad looked down at him, troubled, and said,

"If I had need of company, be sure that I would not refuse you."

"I would be to you the best squire in Christendom," said the boy.

And Sir Galahad said, "But I ask of you a harder thing."

"I will do anything!"

"Then go back to the abbey, and be with King Bagdemagus while he mends of his wound, that Sir Owain may be free to follow his quest."

And the squire ceased his pleading and rose from his knees. "I will do the harder thing," he said, though the words choked within him.

And so they parted.

Sir Galahad rode for many days, wherever the forest took him, and without meeting any other adventure, until one morning he came out on to the slopes of a broad and pleasant valley through which a river wound its shining way; and saw in front of him a castle, tall and turreted, that seemed to float above its own reflection in the water, as a swan will do. As he sat his horse, looking down towards it, an old ragged man came by, and gave him God's greeting in the passing. Galahad returned the greeting, and asked the name of the castle.

"Sir, it is called the Castle of Maidens," said the old man.

"That is a fair name."

"Maybe so, but it casts a dark shadow on the land."

"How is that?" asked Sir Galahad.

"Because of its custom. Its evil treatment of those who pass by. Better that you turn back and follow another way."

"I do not like to turn from my chosen road," said

Galahad, "but assuredly I shall not pass by." And he flicked the reins, and rode on, making sure of his weapons as he went, while the old man, wagging his head and grumbling to himself about the rashness of youth, hobbled on into the forest.

When Galahad drew near to the castle, a mounted page came out to meet him, and bending his wild-eyed mare side-on across the track, demanded to know his business, in the name of the lords of the castle.

"I seek only to learn the custom of this place," said Sir Galahad peaceably.

"Bide here, and truly you may learn it, and find the lesson little to your taste," said the page insolently, and, making his mare dance and snort, he wheeled about and rode full gallop back to the castle.

Galahad sat his horse in the dust of the track and waited, and in a little while there burst out from the castle seven armed and splendidly mounted knights, who shouted to him, as with one voice, "Sir knight, put up your guard, for the answer to the question that you ask is death!"

And all seven together, they set their lances in rest and came charging straight down upon him.

Sir Galahad pricked forward to meet them, and felled the firstcomer with a blow that came near to breaking his neck. Six more lance points rang against his shield, but he remained as firm as ever in the saddle, and the shield was not even scratched, though the weight of the thrusts flung his horse back on its haunches. He flung aside his own splintered lance, and drew his sword, and the fight went on; one against seven, so that the seven thought to have an easy victory. Yet it seemed that the lone knight did not know how to tire, and their weapons could not scathe him; and when the fight had raged till noon, and the seven were all sore wounded and weary beyond lifting sword arm, a cold fear fell upon their hearts, and they turned and fled.

Galahad sat his weary horse to watch them go; and when the dusk had sunk behind them, he turned to the castle bridge; and there in the gateway stood an old man in the habit of a priest, who held out to him a bunch of massive keys.

"Sir," said the old man, "this castle is yours now, by right of conquest, and all within it, to do with as you will."

So Galahad rode into the castle; and as soon as he was within the walls, a great crowd of maidens came thronging about him, many-voiced and fluttering as bright birds in a cage, crying, "Welcome! Sir knight, we have waited long and long for one to come who could free us from our captivity!"

And while some took his horse, others led him to the inner court, and helped him to unarm as though they had been his squire. And when he was unhelmed, a maiden tall and fair beyond all the rest came out through an inner door, carrying an ivory horn, wonderfully carved and bound about with gold. She held the horn out to Sir Galahad, saying, "Gentle sir, let you sound this, to summon all the knights who will hold their lands from you, now that you are lord of this castle. Then, when they are gathered here before you, let you have them swear on the crosses of their swords that the old evil custom of this place shall never return to it again."

Sir Galahad took the horn, and stood with it in his hands. "First, do you tell me what custom that is; and why so many maidens are captive here."

The old priest took up the story.

"Ten years ago, the knights who today you vanquished and put to flight came to this castle asking hospitality of Duke Lynoor, the lord of all these parts. Now the Duke had two daughters; and as soon as they saw them, these same knights would each and every one have had the eldest and most beautiful for his lady. So there burst out a great quarrel among the knights and between them and the Duke. And the Duke and his son were slain, and the maidens made captive. Then the knights having other things to think of, ceased their quarrel among themselves and made common cause to seize the castle treasure, and summoning all the fighting men of these parts, they fell to waging war on their neighbours, until they had forced them all to submit and become their vassals. Then the Duke's elder daughter said to them, 'In truth, my lords, as this castle was captured because of a maiden, so, because of other maidens, it shall be lost again; and one knight shall be the downfall of seven.'

"At this, the seven knights were greatly enraged. And from that day forward, in revenge for her words, and also that none should have the chance to bring them true, they have taken and held captive every maiden to pass beneath the castle walls."

"And the Duke's daughters?" said Galahad, and looked towards the maiden who had brought him the ivory horn.

"Nay," said the maiden, "my sister is dead long since. I was but a child when they came."

Then Sir Galahad set the horn to his lips and winded a call that sent the echoes flying ten forest leagues away.

Presently, men came from far and wide to answer the

summons. And when all were gathered, he said to the Duke's younger daughter, "Lady, this castle is mine by right of conquest, to do with as I will. So now I make a gift of it to you."

And he caused all the assembled knights to swear fealty to her, and to take oath upon the crosses of their swords, that never again should the old evil customs return to the castle, and that all the captive maidens should at once be set free and sent in safety to their own homes.

And that night he supped and slept in the castle, which was no longer called the Castle of Maidens; and next morning after hearing Mass, he rode out again on his way.

But now the story leaves Sir Galahad a while, and tells of Sir Lancelot.

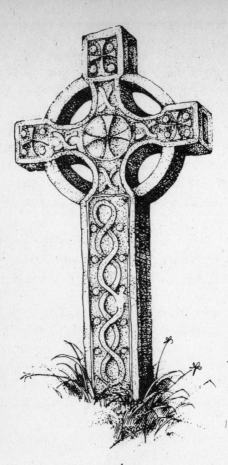

4

SIR LANCELOT
FAILS HIS TESTING

For many days after parting from his companions, Sir
Lancelot rode alone through the forest, waiting with an
open heart for God to tell him what to do and whither
to turn his horse's head. But indeed it seemed to him
that in that forest there was neither time nor place, so
that a man might ride many days towards the sunset,

and find himself at the last back in the place from which he had set out; almost, he might bide quiet beneath a tree and let the forest shift around him, like the country of a dream.

And then one morning he came down to a stream, and found a big warhorse that he thought he knew grazing on the bank, its bit slipped free and its reins carefully knotted up to be out of its way. And sitting with his back to an alder tree, helmet off and his yellow head tipped back against the rough bark, Sir Percival, whistling soft and full-throated to a blackbird, and the blackbird whistling back as though they were old friends. But, indeed, Sir Percival was friends with all furred and feathered things.

He got to his feet when he saw Sir Lancelot ride out from the woodshore, slowly, as men move in armour, and they greeted each other; and when Sir Lancelot had turned his own horse loose to graze beside the other, they sat down again together beneath the alder tree. And Percival asked if he had seen or heard anything of Sir Galahad.

"Neither sound nor sight," said Lancelot.

Percival sighed.

"Were you seeking him?"

"I was hoping we might ride together a little while," Percival said, "but it was a foolish hope."

It seemed to Lancelot that the knight beside him was young to be riding errant and alone in the dark forest. And yet that was foolishness, for Percival had shown himself in the jousting to be no green boy. He was older than Galahad by at least a year, and no one would be thinking Galahad young to ride errant, no matter through what dark forest.

"Would I serve, until we can come by word of Sir Galahad?" he said. There was a smile in his voice; and if it was a crooked smile, that was hidden in the shadow of his helmet.

And Percival said, "If it be not Sir Galahad, there is none that I would rather ride with."

So when they went on again, they rode together.

For many days they kept each other company, and then one evening, in a wild dark country of rocks and twisted low-growing trees, they met with a knight bearing a great white shield blazoned with a blood-red cross; and because the device was strange to them, they did not know him for Sir Galahad, lately come from freeing the Castle of Maidens.

Sir Lancelot called out to him to know his name, but Sir Galahad never answered, for indeed he was away inside himself in some desert solitude of his own, as was often the way with him, and had no thought to come back and greet and be greeted by other men.

So when he did not answer, but would have ridden on across their path, Sir Lancelot called out a warning; and when still he neither checked nor answered, shouted the final challenge, "Joust!" and couching his lance, rode straight at him. Galahad looked round, then, and swung his horse to meet the charge; and the lance took him full on the shield and shattered into a score of pieces; but he remained rock-firm in the saddle, and his own lance in the same instant took Sir Lancelot under the guard, and hove him clean over his horse's crupper, but did him no other harm. Then Percival came thundering down upon the unknown knight, but Sir Galahad wrenched his horse aside, and as the other missed his thrust, took him with the sideways lance stroke as he hurtled past, and swept him from the saddle, so that he plunged down all asprawl beside Sir Lancelot, not knowing if it was day or night.

And Sir Galahad went back to the solitude within himself, and turned his horse and rode away.

By the time the two he had felled had gathered themselves together and caught their horses and remounted, he was long out of sight.

"We have no hope of catching him now," said Percival, "and this wilderness of rocks is no good place for us, with the dusk coming down. Let us turn back to the hermitage we passed a while since, and beg shelter for the night." For truth to tell, his bruises ached.

But Sir Lancelot was in a deeper pain. For this was the first time since he took valour that ever he had been unhorsed. And again, and achingly, he was remembering the words on Galahad's sword. Two things were most dear to him in life; one was his love for the Queen, and one was knowing that he was the best knight in the world; not merely the strongest, but the best, and not only that other men should say it of him, but that he should know it of himself. And the knowledge was beginning to grow most painfully within him that of these two things, he could not have both.

Sir Percival felt the trouble in his companion, and said, quick and warm, "It was surely a chance stroke."

Lancelot shook his head, "It was as clean a fall as ever I saw one knight give another. That is why I must press on after him. I must know who he is—"

"Wait until morning," Percival said, "and then we will seek him together."

"No," said Lancelot, "I must know—I must find out—"

"Then God go with you," said Percival, "but I will ride no further this night."

So they parted, and Percival turned back to the hermitage, while Lancelot pushed on through the rocks and the stunted trees and the gathering dusk, after the glimmer of a crimson cross on a white shield.

When it was full dark, he came to a rough stone cross that stood on the edge of wild heath country at the parting of two ways; and close beyond it saw an ancient chapel. He dismounted, and, leading his horse, walked towards the chapel, for he hoped there might be someone there who could tell him which way the knight had gone. But when he had looped the reins over a branch of the ancient hawthorn that grew beside the place, and turned himself to look more closely at the chapel, it was no more than a ruin, with nettles growing thick about the door sill; and coming within the porch, he found a rusty iron grille to bar his way.

And yet the place could not be deserted after all, for light flooded out to him through the grille, and within, he could see an altar richly hung with silken cloths; and before the altar, six candles glimmered crocus-flamed in a branched silver candlestick. But no man moved within the lighted sanctuary—nothing stirred save the night wind blowing from the heath; and though a great longing came upon him to go in and kneel before the altar, there was no way in. No way at all.

For a long time he knelt there outside the grille, hoping that someone would come, but no one came, and at last he rose and turned away, and unhitching his horse from the thorn branch, led it back as far as the wayside cross, unsaddled it and turned it loose to graze. Then he unlaced his helm and set it on the ground, unbuckled his sword belt, and lying down with his head on his shield, fell into a fitful sleep full of ragged dreams and uneasy wakings, and always the vision of the knight with the white shield glimmering far ahead of him, out of reach.

By and by, as he lay so, a late moon began to rise; and by its light he saw coming towards him along the track two palfreys with a litter slung between them; and in the litter a knight, sick or wounded, and moaning aloud in his pain. The mounted squire who led the foremost palfrey halted close beside the cross. And the knight broke out from his dumb moaning into piteous words: "Sweet God in Heaven, shall my sufferings never cease? Shall I never see the Holy Cup which shall ease this weary pain?" And he stretched out his hands in anguished pleading.

And all the while, Sir Lancelot lay without speech or movement, so that he seemed to be asleep, yet seeing all that went on. And lying so, he saw the silver candle-stick issue from the chapel, no hand carrying it, and with its six tapers burning clear and still, move towards the cross. And behind the candles, floating in the same way, lightly as a fallen leaf floats on still water, came a silver table; and on the table, half veiled in its own light, so that his eyes could not fully look upon it, the Grail that he had seen in Arthur's court at the feast of Pentecost.

No thunder this time, no sunbeam, but the great stillness, and the blaze of white light.

And when he saw the wonder coming towards him, the sick knight tumbled himself from his litter, and lay where he fell, his hands stretched out to it, crying, "Lord, look on me in thy mercy, and by the power of this holy vessel grant me healing from my sickness!"

And with his eyes fixed upon the light, he dragged himself towards it, until he could touch the silver table with his hands. And even as he did so, a great shudder ran through him, and he gave a sobbing and triumphant cry, "Ah, God! I am healed!"

And with that cry, it was as though he sank into sleep.

And all the while, in his strange half-waking state, Sir Lancelot saw and heard, yet could feel *nothing*. He watched the Grail come, and stay a while, and presently move back into the chapel again; and he knew that it was the Grail of his quest, and his heart should have leapt in awe and exultation, and he should have been kneeling in worship beside the other knight; and still he could feel *nothing*. It was as though his spirit within him was turned to lead.

When the Grail was gone back into the chapel again, and the six-branched candlestick after it, and there was no light but the moon, the knight of the litter awoke, strong again and filled with life as though he had never known a day's sickness; and his squire came from where he had been waiting at a little distance all the while, and said, "Sir, is it well with you?"

"It is well and more than well with me, thanks be to God!" said the knight. "But I cannot but wonder how it is with yonder man who lies sleeping at the foot of the cross, and did not rouse once at the marvel that has been here this night."

"Surely it must be some wretch who has committed a great sin, so that God deemed him unworthy of the mystery that you have been allowed to share," said the squire.

And he brought the knight's armour, which had lain

beside him in the litter, and helped him to arm. But when it came to the helm, the squire came across to where Sir Lancelot lay, and took up his helm, and his sword Joyeux that lay beside him, and caught and saddled his horse, and took all to his master. "You will make better use of these, for sure," said he, "than that worthless knight who must have forfeited all right to such honourable gear. Now mount, my lord, and let us ride."

So the knight mounted Sir Lancelot's horse, and the squire again leading the litter palfreys, they rode away.

Soon after, Sir Lancelot stirred and sat up, like a man rousing from deep sleep; and at first he wondered whether he had indeed seen, or only dreamed, what had happened. Then he got up and went back to the chapel. But the grille was still across the doorway, and though the tapers glimmered within, he could see no sign of the Grail.

For a while he stood there, waiting, he did not know for what, and hoping—hoping— And then there came a voice from somewhere, maybe out of his own heart. It was a cold and terrible voice that said, "Lancelot, harder than stone, more bitter than wood, more barren than the fig tree, get thee gone from this holy place, for thy presence fouls it."

And he turned away, and stumbled back to the foot of the wayside cross, weeping as he went, for what he had lost without ever finding it. And so he saw that his horse and sword and helm were gone, and he knew that it was all bitter truth and none of it a dream. And he crouched down at the foot of the cross, and came near to breaking his heart within him.

The day dawned at last, sun up, and the sky ringing

with lark-song above the open country. Sir Lancelot had always taken great joy in such mornings; but now he felt that nothing could ever bring him joy again; and he turned away from the wayside cross and the chapel and the open heathland, and set out again through the dark forest, unhorsed and unhelmed, and with his sword sheath hanging empty at his side.

The day was still short of noon when he came upon a small wattle-built woodland church, in which a solitary priest was making ready for the service. He went in and knelt down, and heard Mass; and when it was over, begged the priest for council, in the name of God.

"What manner of council do you seek?" asked the holy man. "Is it that you would make your confession?"

"I have sore need to do that," said Lancelot.

"Come then, in the name of God."

He led him to the altar, and the two of them knelt down side by side.

Then the priest asked Lancelot his name, and when he heard that the stranger with the crooked grief-stricken face was Sir Lancelot of the Lake, he said, "Then, sir, if all I have heard of the foremost of Arthur's knights be true, you owe God a great return, for that he has made you the man you are."

"Then ill have I repaid him," said Lancelot, "and this he has all too clearly shown me, in the thing that befell me last night."

"Tell me of last night," said the priest.

And Sir Lancelot told him of all that had passed.

When he had finished, the priest said, "Now it is clear to me that you bear the weight of some mortal sin upon your soul. But the Lord God holds out his arms to all sinners who repent and make amendment. Now therefore make your confession to God, through me, and I will give you all the help and counsel that I may."

But Lancelot knelt there silent, with bowed head. He had made his confession as often as any other man. But he had never made it fully; for the love between himself and the Queen was not his alone to confess. Yet he knew in his heart that it was the thing that was shutting him out from God. He had never known that so clearly as he knew it now, and his heart was torn two ways. And still the priest begged him to confess his sin, promising that if he did so and renounced it utterly God would let him in again. And at last it was as though something cracked within him, and he said like a man in mortal pain, "For more than twenty years I have loved my Lady Guenever, the Queen."

"And you have won her love to you?"

Lancelot bowed his head lower yet.

"And what of King Arthur, her lord?"

"The marriage was made between them for the good of the kingdom, after the way of marriages between kings and queens. After, she grew to love him as a most dear friend. To me also he is the best-loved friend I have ever had. We would not that any hurt should come to him."

"Yet you wrong him by your love for each other, every hour of every day."

"I am a great sinner," said Sir Lancelot, "and the weight of my sin is on my head and on my spirit. I am shut out from God."

"So then, your sin is confessed," said the priest. "Now swear before God, as you hope for his forgiveness, that you will turn from the Queen's fellowship, and never be with her again, save when others are by."

"I swear," said Sir Lancelot, seeming to tear something raw and bleeding from his breast.

"And that from now on, you will not even wish for her presence, nor be with her in your inmost thoughts," said the priest; and his words fell single and pitiless as axe blows.

"I—swear," said Sir Lancelot. But he prayed within himself, "God help me! For unless you help me, I have sworn an oath which I cannot keep. I will try, with all the strength that is in me. More, I cannot do. And sweet God in Heaven, help and comfort my lady also." And so he was already a little foresworn.

Then the priest gave him absolution and his blessing.

And they rose from before the altar, and turned to leave the church. And seeing how the knight stumbled as though for mortal weariness, the holy man said, "My cell is close by; come with me and rest, and when you are rested, we will speak of what is next for you to do."

"I thank you; and glad would I be to rest," said Lancelot. "As to what is next for me to do, that I already know; I must find some way to come by another sword and helm and another horse, that I may ride forward again on the Quest."

"In that I can help you," said the priest, "for I have a brother, a knight-at-arms, rich in this world's goods, who lives not far from here. And he will furnish all these things gladly, as soon as I send to ask for them."

"Then my thanks to you, and to your brother. And most surely I will stay a while."

And now the story leaves Sir Lancelot of the Lake, and tells again of Sir Percival.

5

SIR PERCIVAL:
KINGS AND DEMONS

When Percival left Sir Lancelot to ride on alone, he
went back to the hermitage, and the holy woman who
lived there gave him shelter for the night. And in the
morning when they had prayed together, and she had
fed him on black bread spread with golden honey from
her own bees, he buckled on his armour and rode out
again.

All day he rode, through a wild country of rocks and blackened heathland and dark drought-stunted trees, along the fringes of King Pelles' Waste Land; and all day long he met never a soul. But towards evening he heard the deep tolling of a bell, a warm bronze sound, a sound with a bloom on it like the bloom on dark grapes, summoning through the trees. And he made his way towards it, hoping for shelter for that night also.

Almost at once he came to a large abbey, ringed around with walls that looked as though they were meant to keep out the world. But when he sat his horse before the gate and shouted cheerfully, the monks came running to open it and make him welcome. They took his horse to the stables and himself to a fair guest chamber; and there he supped and slept; and when he woke, the bell was ringing again, for it was the morning hour of Prime. He got up and went quickly to the abbey church, where the brethren were already gathered, to hear Mass.

Midway up the church there was an ironwork screen, and beyond it the Mass priest was making ready. Percival went towards it, expecting to pass through and join the rest. But there seemed to be no gate in the screen. So he knelt down outside it, and looking through saw beyond the Mass priest a bed richly spread with silken coverings, all of the purest white. Someone lay on the bed, under the coverings; but in the shadows he could not make out whether it was a man or a woman. And then the thought came to him that he was not there for staring and wondering, and he set himself to listen to the Mass.

But when the priest held up the Host, the figure on the bed sat up, and Percival saw that it was an ancient man, his hair as white as the silken coverings, and on his head a golden crown. As the coverings fell away, he showed naked to the hips, and his body and face and arms were striped with wounds and gashes enough to have killed three men. When he stretched out his hands towards the Host, even the palms of his hands were wounded.

He cried out, "Most gracious and loving Father, be not unmindful of my dues!" and remained sitting with his hands stretched out, until Mass was over and the priest brought him the communion bread. And after that he lay down again under the white silken coverings, and was as he had been before.

Percival was filled with compassion and curiosity. He followed the brethren when they came by some side way from behind the screen, and outside, in the cloisters, he drew the one he thought had the kindest face apart, and said, "If it is not unseemly of me to ask, let you tell me of the old wounded man with the gold crown upon his head who lies beside the altar."

"Gladly I will tell you," said the monk, who had told the story many times before, but still found it painful and still a marvel in the telling. "That is King Mordrain of the city of Sarras, over beyond the Holy Land." And he told Percival of Joseph of Arimathea and his son Josephus, and King Mordrain, and the great white shield with its blood-red cross, just as the White Knight had told it to Sir Galahad. And he told also, how, after the battle to free Joseph and his people from the wicked British king, when they came to unarm King Mordrain, they found him covered with wounds enough to kill three men, but he swore that he felt no pain and all was well with him.

day," said the monk, "the Christians gathered
e Holy Grail to make their prayers and thanks-
givings. And King Mordrain, who since he became a
Christian had longed above all things to enter into the
mystery of the Grail, drew too near. Then a voice in
their midst, and no man speaking, said, 'King, go no
closer. It is forbidden thee.' But the King's longing was
so great that still, as the service of the Grail went on, he
drew by little and little nearer yet.

"And suddenly the brightness of the Grail engulfed
him; and he fell to the ground. And when he awoke, as
if from a swoon, there was neither strength in his limbs
nor sight in his eyes.

"Then he prayed, 'Gracious Lord Jesus Christ, I
would have looked upon that which you forbade me;
and this punishment is just, and I accept it willingly.
Yet grant me this, that I may not die until that knight
born of the line of Arimathea, he that is to enter at last
into the mystery of the Grail, shall come to set me free.'

"And the voice said, 'King, Our Lord has heard thy
prayer, and it is granted. When the knight Galahad
comes to thee, thy sight shall be restored that thou shalt
see him clear; and thy wounds shall be healed that will
not close before; and thou shalt be set free.'

"Then King Mordrain ordered that his shield with
the blazon of the blood-red cross upon it should be
taken and lodged at a certain abbey where it was told
him in a dream that the knight Galahad should come for
it, five days after he received knighthood.

"And for four hundred years, he has lain as you saw
him but now, touching no food but that which the priest
brings to him at the sacrament of the Mass, and waiting
for the knight who bears his own shield to set him free."

"That has been a long waiting time," said Percival, in awe.

"But now it seems that it is nearly over, for word has come that the shield has been claimed, and its new master has been seen carrying it in the forest."

And Percival saw again in his memory the knight who had unhorsed both himself and Sir Lancelot, two days since; and the last level light of sunset burning on the blood-red cross of his shield. And so he knew who the knight was, and could have wept that he had not known before.

"Now he is two days ahead of me," he thought. And he was in such desperate haste to be gone that he would not even wait to eat with the brethren, but begged for his horse and armour, and giving them courteous but hurried thanks and farewell, mounted and rode away, his morning shadow out ahead of him like an eager hound in leash.

About noon, the track that he was following led down into a wooded valley; and there he saw coming towards him a score of armed men.

And as they drew towards each other, the foremost of the band called out to him to know his name and fealty.

"I am called Percival of Wales, and my fealty is to King Arthur."

As soon as they heard this, they shouted, "Have at him!" one taking up the cry from another, and, ripping out their swords, thrust their horses forward against him.

Percival's own sword seemed to leap from its sheath into his hand, as he made ready to meet them. But they were twenty to his one, for all the skill and swiftness of his swordplay. His horse was killed under him, and as he sprang clear, he was beaten to his knees, and the blows crashed in on him from all sides, gashing through his helm and shoulder mail. A few more panting breaths of time, and it would have been all over with him. But as the struggle began to darken before his eyes, suddenly, as an ill dream flies at waking, the yelling press about him broke and crumbled; and above him, high on his great horse, he saw a knight whose sword seemed kin for swiftness to the summer lightning, and whose white shield blazed with the blood-red cross it bore.

The enemy knights were scattered and galloping for the shelter of the forest. And as young Percival, sobbing for breath, his head swimming inside his hacked and battered helmet, struggled to his feet and turned to thank his rescuer, the knight of the red-cross shield struck spurs to his horse and was gone also, making in the opposite direction, as one who has done what he came to do, and has nothing more to stay for.

Percival shouted after him, desperately, "Sir knight! For God's sweet sake let you stay and speak with me!"

But the other showed no sign of having heard. Only a flicker of red and white showed for an instant through the stunted trees, and then was gone into the brown glooms of the forest. The beat of horse-hooves died away. Somewhere a jay gave its alarm call, and then all was still.

Percival stood where he was, his moment of incredulous joy chilling to despair. Blood from the wound in his head trickled into his eyes, and his heart felt as though it must burst his breast-cage. Then, having no horse, he began to run, like a child running desperately after his heart's desire.

For a long time he ran, blundering against trees,

falling into the hollows where the old and rotten forest floor gave way beneath him, sobbing as he ran, long after he knew that it was no use to run any further. Until at last he fell headlong over a hidden root, and pitching down onto the wound in his head, knocked himself dizzy. There he lay still, and heard the silence of the forest all about him, save for the mocking laughter of a green woodpecker somewhere among the trees.

Then he tore off the wreck of his helmet, and flung aside sword and shield, and fell to the sorest weeping that ever he had known, until at last, forsaken and desperate and with an aching head, he wept himself to sleep.

When he awoke, it was far into the night, and the moon was riding high and cold and uncaring above the tangled branches. And a woman was bending over him.

"Percival." Her voice was soft and warm on the lonely places of his mind. "Percival, what are you doing here?"

He was too confused and miserable even to wonder how she knew his name. He was grateful that she sounded kind, and that was all. "Alas, I do nothing," he said, sitting up and getting slowly to his feet. "And truth to tell, lady, if I had not lost my horse, I would not be here at all."

"If you would promise to do my bidding whenever I call on you," said the lady, "I could find you a horse; one that has no equal for fire or beauty or speed of foot."

Hope leapt in Percival. "As to that, I am a knight, and one of Arthur's court, and so sworn to be the true and faithful servant of all women who need my help."

"Wait for me, then, and in a little I will return."

And suddenly, she was not there any more.

Percival did think it a little odd that he had not seen her go; but it was very dark under the trees; and before he had had time to do much thinking, she was back. And she was leading a great warhorse, black as sin itself from proud crest to sweeping tail. Its round hooves trampled the forest floor as though it scorned the earth beneath it, and there was a fire in its eye that Percival had never seen in even the most mettlesome horse before. For as long as he could remember, all horses and all hounds had been his friends, and he had never known what it was to fear even the wildest of them. But at sight of this one, something shot through him that he thought was fear, though in truth it was a shaft of warning. Still, it was a horse, and a fine fleet one, and the thing he most needed in all the world, just then. So he sheathed his sword and laced on his battered helm again and catching up his shield, swung into the high saddle and settled his feet in the stirrups with a reckless joy.

"Go now," said the lady, "but remember what you have promised me."

"I will remember," said Sir Percival, not at all sure what he *had* promised. "My thanks to you, lady."

And he struck spurs to the horse's flanks, and felt the surge of pride and power beneath him as the great beast bounded forward.

Then began the wildest ride that ever was ridden by mortal knight.

They were off and away at full gallop, crashing through the trees, faster and faster. Low, hanging branches tried to sweep Sir Percival from the saddle, the ground was a dark blur that fled backwards beneath the pounding hooves; and when he would have reined in something of their headlong pace, the black horse snorted and leapt forward against the bit. And then it seemed to the young knight that they were no longer galloping at all but borne upon the air. On and on over hills and valleys, the night rushing past on either hand. The forest was behind them now, and it seemed to Percival that they must have covered many days of distance in that wild midnight ride. On and on, the foam flying back like spindrift from the black muzzle, the wind of their going screaming by. And then ahead of them was a wide and rushing river; and the black horse neighed in triumph, making straight towards it. Now indeed Percival thought the moment of his death was upon him, and desperately put his hand to his forehead and made the sign of the cross.

And in that instant, feeling the weight of the cross upon it, the thing that wore the shape of a black horse gave itself a violent shake, and flung its rider from the saddle; and so plunged into the flood, howling and shrieking as it went; and instead of spray, bright sheaves of flame shot up on either side of it, as though the river itself were on fire.

And sprawling on the bank where he had fallen, Percival gave thanks to God, who had saved his soul from damnation.

When morning broke, and he could look about him, there was no sign of the river at all; no sign of the country of his wild night ride. He was on a rocky island, girt about on all sides by sea; and the sea stretching away to the sky's edge with no other sight of land. There was no trace anywhere of men and women, no dwelling places nor cultivated land; but the island was not empty of life, for wherever he looked among the tawny rocks prowled the striped and speckled shapes of wild beasts;

lions and leopards and strange winged serpents.

"Now I am in deadly peril of another kind," thought Percival, and felt for his sword, and then he saw that in the very middle of the island a great crag thrust heavenward. If he could reach the crest of it, the sheer rock-faces below might be some protection against attack from the wild animals. So, at the best speed he could make, he set off towards it.

But as he began the climb, the most terrible uproar broke upon his ears, and a vast shadow swept between him and the sun; and looking up, he saw one of the great winged serpents with a lion cub in its jaws, making for the rocky summit like an eagle carrying home its kill. But the cub was still alive, and crying out in terror, and hard behind came a lioness, tearing the day apart with her roaring, and striving to leap into the air after the winged horror, desperate to save her young.

Percival began to run, drawing his sword as he went, but the lioness passed him and was first to gain the crest; and when he also reached it, lioness and serpent were locked in battle, she tearing at the monster's throat, the scaly tail tightening about her body. Percival ran in among the lashing coils and caught the creature a glancing blade-blow on the head, at which it rounded on him, spewing out great gobbets of flame. He sprang aside, then thrust in again. The struggle was long and desperate; but at last his sword found a second time the place on its head where the first blow had landed. There the scaly hide was laid open and the bone cracked, and the second blow broke the slim, savage head apart, and the great coils ceased to lash, and the fire sank away, as the monster dropped dead at his feet.

Then Sir Percival sheathed his sword and flung aside

his scorched shield, and pulled off his helmet to feel the cool wind on his head. And the lioness, when she had made sure that all was well with her cub, came and fawned on him like a great dog, bending her proud neck against his knee, her tail sweeping behind her in gratitude and delight. And Percival fell to stroking her head and shoulders.

"The Lord does not mean that I should be lonely in this place, for he has sent you to keep me company."

All day the lioness stayed with him, until, when dusk came, she took the cub by the scruff of its neck, and bounded away down the steep slopes to her lair in some place unknown to him among the rocks. Then the young knight was very desolate, thinking that she had deserted him, and feeling himself now quite alone. But before the dusk had deepened into the dark, having seen the cub safely lodged and fed, she returned to him, friendlywise as before, and lay down beside him. And Percival put his arm round her neck and fondled behind her ears as he would have done to a favourite hound, while she rubbed her head against him. And at last he propped himself against her, his head on her flank for a pillow, more glad of her company than almost ever he had been of company before. And so he fell asleep.

When he woke in the morning, the lioness was gone; but looking out to sea, he beheld a ship with sails spread like dark wings, flying straight as an arrow towards the island.

Hope leapt in Percival, for surely a ship must mean the promise of rescue, and he caught up helm and sword and shield, and went scrambling and leaping down through the rocks towards the shore.

Even as he went, he kept his gaze on the ship winging

in towards him. And surely she was the strangest vessel that ever man saw, for she came as though all the four winds of heaven were in her sails, and ahead of her raced a whirlwind that parted the waters and beat up great waves curling back from her on either side. And as she drew close in to the land, he saw that she was clad from stem to stern with draperies that formed a pavilion of fine black silk. She slackened speed as the wind dropped from her sails, and settled lightly as a bird against the shore where the rocks rose straight from deep water. And Percival, reaching the shore at the same moment, saw that seated in the black-draped entrance amidships was the most beautiful maiden he had ever beheld, with a mouth as silken red as harvest poppies, and eyes and hair as dark as midnight.

Just for a moment he thought that he had seen such blackness somewhere not long ago; but he could not think where. And the maiden was holding out her hands to him, saying in a voice as sweet as wild-wood honey, "Sir knight, how come you to be here on this island, so far from the haunts of men that but for the chance wind that has brought me to your aid, you must surely have died of hunger or been slain by wild beasts before any help could find you?"

"That is a long story that I scarcely know myself," said Percival, "but I think that whatever happens to me, it is God's will."

The lady made a movement with her hands, as though to brush something aside, and she laughed a little. "Then it must be by God's will that the winds blew me here, Sir Percival of Wales."

"You know my name!" said Percival, surprised.

"I know it well, I know you better than you think."

"Then if you know so much of me, grant that I may know something of you."

"Know then," said she, "that I am one who would have been the greatest lady in my land, if I had not been wrongfully driven from it."

Instantly pity and indignation rose in Percival, and he said, "Damsel in exile, tell me who has used you so cruelly."

"A great lord," she said, "a mighty king who chose me for my beauty and placed me in his household. For I was beautiful; more beautiful than you see me now with my sorrows come upon me. And being so fair, alas, I grew a little vain and spoiled, and spoke to my lord one day foolishly and light-heartedly in a manner that he took amiss, though indeed there was little harm in it. Then his wrath flared out against me as though I had done some monstrous ill, and he drove me forth with a few who were loyal to me, into exile. And now, that by the wind's chance I have found you, who I know to be a valiant and honourable knight, I beg you to help me against this cruel lord who has so misused me. Indeed, you cannot refuse me, for you are of the Round Table, and so bound by your oath, sworn there at King Arthur's bidding, to be the champion of all distressed ladies who ask your aid."

"Indeed I am bound by that oath, but even if I were not, still would I give you all the help in my power," said Percival.

And she thanked him very sweetly; and they sat talking for a while, she on the deck of her ship and he on the rocks alongside.

Noon came and the sun beat down, and the rocks gave back their heat in shimmering waves; and Percival felt like to fry inside his armour, but was too courteous to tell the lady so.

But at last, of her own accord, she turned behind her into the ship, and spoke to someone out of sight, and two servants brought out a tent of black silk lined with crimson, and set it up on a small patch of shore-grass, very pretty to see, with every silken edge of canopy and curtains dagged like black flower petals, and little gay pennants that fluttered overall. And when all was ready, and the curtains looped back to let every movement of air pass through, she called to Percival, "Come now, and sit here with me in the shade, for it is too hot out there on the bare rocks."

So Percival came; and in the blissful coolth of the shade under the awning, she helped him to unharness, and bathed his hurts, crying out softly at sight of them, and he lay down on soft cushions and slept.

When he woke, a low table had been set up beside him, and the servants were bringing food from the ship; the most choice and delicate of food in bowls and dishes of such intricate beauty that he could scarce believe they had been made by human hands.

"Eat with me," said the lady. And Sir Percival sat up and thanked her, and began to eat, he on one side of the table and she on the other, their eyes often meeting. Then the servants brought cool wine clouding in crystal goblets; and it was such wine as Percival had never drunk before, and went to his head like no wine that he had ever drunk before; so that soon he began to see everything through a golden haze. And the lady seemed kinder and more beautiful with every moment that went by. And when he stretched his hand to meet hers across the table, it was the softest thing that he had ever touched, and her fingers curled round his so that his heart turned over in his breast for the sweetness of the moment.

"Love me," said the lady. "It is so long since any loved me, and I am sorely alone."

"I will be the truest lover to you that ever lady had," said Percival.

And the table was no longer between them, but she was beside him on the couch of soft cushions. But even as he put his arms round her to draw her close, it happened that Sir Percival's eye fell upon the hilt of his sword, where he had laid it down beside him, and as with all knightly swords, it formed a cross.

Instantly the golden haze turned grey, and a cold and shuddering fear seized upon him. Desperately he fumbled one hand to his forehead and crossed himself; and as he did so, a great howling and shrieking broke out all around; and he was choked by a filthy stench that had caught him by the throat. The tent collapsed into bat-wing tatters, and all things seemed whirling away into nothingness. And he cried out like one drowning, "Lord Jesus Christ, help me or I am lost!"

He found that his eyes were clenched shut, and when he opened them, he was lying among the baking rocks, and of the tent and the soft cushions, the food and the servants, there was no sign. But looking seaward, he saw the black-draped ship putting off from the shore; and in the entrance where he had seen her first stood the lady. But now all her beauty and sweetness were gone, and she screamed at him, "Percival, you have betrayed me!"

Then the ship was racing out to sea, with such a storm springing up in her wake that it seemed at any moment she must founder, and the whole sea aflame to engulf her. But before the flames and the tempest the black ship sped on her way faster than any wind could blow.

Percival watched until ship and storm were out of sight, then sank down on his knees, weeping most bitterly, and thanking God for his deliverance and praying for forgiveness, and then weeping again for shame and misery and near despair.

All that night he passed on the rocky shore, not even caring now if the wild beasts of the island came and killed him. But none came near. Nor did his lioness come to comfort him, and he supposed that he was no longer worthy of her. It seemed the longest and darkest night that ever he had known.

But dawn came at last, and with the dawn he saw another ship making into land; a very different vessel, with sails of white samite, gliding in among the rocks as quietly as a swan on calm water. And when he got up and went to look closer, there was no one on board. But as he stood marvelling at this, a voice spoke to him out of nowhere.

"Percival, go now aboard this ship, and follow wherever adventure leads thee. And have no fear of anything, for wherever thou goest, God is with thee. Thou hast been near to disaster, but thou hast prevailed, and, therefore, one day thou shalt meet again with Galahad, for whose company thou longest, and with Bors also, for ye are the chosen three."

The voice died into the light shore wind. And Percival took up his arms and went aboard the waiting ship, and pushed off from the rocks; and the wind filled the sails and carried him swiftly out to sea.

But now the story leaves Sir Percival, and tells for a while of Sir Bors.

6

SIR BORS
FIGHTS FOR A LADY

For three days after parting from his companions of the
Round Table, Sir Bors rode through the forest ways
alone. And at evening on the third day he came to a tall,
strong-built tower rising dark against the sunset, in the
midst of a clearing. He beat upon the deep arched gate,
to ask for a night's lodging, and was welcomed in. His
horse was led to the stables and himself up to the Great
Chamber high in the tower, full of honey-golden sunset
light from its western windows that looked away over the
treetops. There he was greeted by the lady of the place,
who was fair and sweet to look upon, but poorly clad
in a patched gown of faded leaf-green silk.

She bade him to sit by her at supper; and when the food was brought in, he saw that it was as poor as her gown, and was sorry for her sake, though for his own it made little difference, for he had taken a vow at the outset, that he would eat no meat and drink no wine while he followed the Quest of the Holy Grail; and so he touched nothing but the bread set before his place, and asked one of the table squires for a cup of water. And seeing this, the lady said, "Ah, sir knight, I know well that the food is poor and rough, but do not disdain it, it is the best we have."

"Lady, forgive me," said Bors, and flushed to the roots of his russet hair, "it is because your food is too good and your wine too rich that I eat bread and drink water, for I have vowed to touch nothing else, while I am on the quest that I follow."

"And what quest is that?"

"The Quest of the Holy Grail."

"I have heard of this quest, and I know you, therefore, for one of King Arthur's knights, the greatest champions in the world," said the lady; and it seemed as though she might have said more, but at that moment a squire came hurrying into the room.

"Madam, it goes ill with us—your sister has taken two more of your castles, and sends you word that she will leave you not one square foot of land, if by tomorrow's noon you have not found a knight to fight for you against her lord!"

Then the lady pressed her hands over her face and wept, until Sir Bors said to her, "Pray you, lady, tell me the meaning of this."

"I will tell you," said the lady. "The lord of these parts once loved my elder sister, never knowing what like she was—what like she is—and by little and little, while they were together, he gave over to her all his power, so that in truth she became the ruler. And her rule was a harsh one, causing the death and maiming and imprisonment of many of his people. Learning wisdom on his deathbed, and listening at last to the distress of his folk, he drove her out and made me his successor in her place, that I might undo what could be undone of the harm. But no sooner was he dead than my sister took a new lord, Priadan the Black, and made alliance with him to wage war on me." She spread her hands. "Good sir, the rest you must know."

"Who and what is this Priadan the Black?" said Bors.

"The greatest champion and the cruellest and most dreaded tyrant in these parts."

"Then send word to your sister, that you have found a knight to fight for you at tomorrow's noon."

Then the lady wept again, for joy. "God give you strength tomorrow," she said, "for it is surely by his sending that you are come here today!"

Next morning, Sir Bors heard Mass in the chapel of the tower, and then went out to the courtyard, where the lady had summoned all the knights yet remaining to her, that they might witness the coming conflict. She would have had him eat before he armed, but he refused, saying that he would fight fasting, and eat after he had fought; and so the squires helped him to buckle on his harness; and he mounted and rode out through the gate, the lady riding a grey palfrey at his side to guide him to the meeting place, and all her people, even to the castle scullions, following after.

They had not ridden far when they came to a level meadow at the head of a valley, and saw a great crowd of people waiting for them, with a fine striped pavilion pitched in their midst. And as they rode out from the long morning shadows of the trees, out from the shadow of the pavilion appeared a damsel in a gown of rose-scarlet damask mounted on a fine bay mare.

"That is my sister," said the lady, "and beside her, look, Priadan, her lord and champion."

The sisters pricked forward to meet each other in the centre of the meadow; and beside the damsel of the pavilion rode a huge knight in armour as black as his tall warhorse; and beside the lady of the tower rode Sir Bors, feeling the balance of his lance.

"Sister," said Sir Bors's lady, "as I sent you word last evening, I have found a champion to fight for my rights, in the matter between us."

"*Rights*!" cried the elder sister. "You played upon my lord when he was in his dotage, until you had wheedled out of him what is truly mine. These are your *rights*!"

"Damsel," said Sir Bors, "your sister has told me the other side of that story. It is she whom I believe, and it is she whom I will fight for this day."

And the two champions looked at each other, each searching out the eye-flicker behind the dark slits of his opponent's helmet.

"Let us waste no more time in talking," said Priadan the Black, "for it was not to talk that we came here."

So the onlookers fell back, leaving a clear space down the midst of the meadow, and the two champions drew apart to opposite ends of it, then wheeled their horses and with levelled lances spurred towards each other. Faster and faster, from canter to full gallop, the spur clods flying from beneath their hooves, until at last they clashed together like two stags battling for the lordship of the herd. Both lances ran true to target, and splintered into kindling wood, and both knights were swept backward over their horses' cruppers to the ground.

With the roar of the crowd like a stormy sea in his ears, Sir Bors was up again on the instant, the Black Knight also. And drawing their swords they fell upon each other with such mighty blows that their shields were soon hacked to rags of painted wood, and the sparks flew from their blades as they rang together and slashed through the mail on flanks and shoulders to set the red blood running. They were so evenly matched that it came to Bors that he must use his head as well as his sword arm, if he was going to carry off the victory. And he began to fight on the defensive, saving his strength and letting his opponent use up his own powers in pressing on to make an end.

The crowd yelled, and the lady he fought for hid her face in her hands. And Sir Bors gave ground a little, and then gave ground again, Priadan pressing after him, until at last he felt the Black Knight beginning to tire, his feet becoming slower, his sword strokes less sure. Then, as though fresh life was suddenly flowing into him, Bors began to press forward in his turn, raining his blows upon the other man, beating him this way and that, until Sir Priadan stumbled like a drunk man, and in the end went over backwards on the trampled turf.

Then Sir Bors bestrode him, and dragged off his helmet and flung it aside, and upswung his sword as though he would have struck Sir Priadan's head from his shoulders and flung it after his helmet.

When Sir Priadan saw the bright arc of the blade above him, he seemed to grow small and grovelling inside his champion's armour, and cried out shrilly, "Quarter! You cannot kill me, I am crying quarter!" And then as Sir Bors still stood over him with menacing sword, "Oh, for God's sweet sake have mercy on me and let me live! I will swear never again to wage war on the lady you serve! I will promise anything you ask, if only you will let me live!"

And Sir Bors lowered his blade, feeling sick, and said, "Remember that oath. And now get out of my sight!"

And the Black Knight scrambled to his feet and made off, running low like a beaten cur.

And the elder sister gave a shrill, furious cry, and set her horse at the onlookers who jostled back to let her by; and so dashed through them and away, rowelling her mare's flanks until the blood on them ran bright as her rose-scarlet gown.

When all those who had come with her and Sir Priadan her lord saw what manner of champion they had followed, they came and swore allegiance to the lady of the tower. And so, with great rejoicing, she and her household rode back the way they had come. And in the Great Chamber of the tower, Sir Bors sat down and ate and drank at last, though still only bread and water; and the lady herself bathed and salved his wounds.

And after he had rested for a day or so, he set out once more on his quest.

And now the story leaves Sir Bors a while, and tells of Sir Gawain.

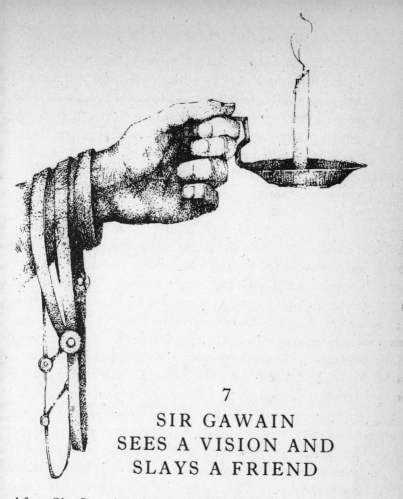

7

SIR GAWAIN
SEES A VISION AND
SLAYS A FRIEND

After Sir Gawain of Orkney left his comrades of the Grail Quest, he wandered from Pentecost until St Magdalen's Day, which is late into July, without ever meeting with any adventure worth the setting down, and it was the same with all his fellows, with whom he crossed paths from time to time. And this he found most odd, for he had expected the Quest for the Holy Grail to provide more strange and marvellous adventures than any quest on which he had ridden before.

Then one day he met with Sir Lancelot's brother, Sir Ector of the Marsh; and that was a fine meeting for both of them, for they were old friends; and gladly they shouted each other's name and beat each other on the shoulders. And when they had done with their greetings, Sir Gawain asked Sir Ector how it went with him.

"Well enough, in body," said Sir Ector, "but I grow weary of riding these forest ways and finding no adventure."

"You too?" cried Sir Gawain. "I swear to you that not one adventure worth the name has come my way since we parted beneath the walls of Camelot. Ten knights have I met and fought with at different times, and ten knights have I slain in fair combat; but there is neither strangeness nor adventure in that."

So they decided that as neither had met with any adventure riding alone, they should ride together for a while, and see if that would change their luck.

And presently, as they rode, Gawain asked his comrade if he had heard any word of Sir Lancelot, his brother.

"No word," said Sir Ector, "it is as though he had ridden out of the world of men; and indeed, my heart is uneasy for him."

"And Galahad, and Percival, and Bors?"

"No word of them either. Those four have vanished, leaving neither wind nor wake behind."

"God guide them, wherever they be," said Sir Gawain.

For a week they rode together, and still met with no adventure. And then towards evening of the seventh day, they came on an ancient chapel. The place was forsaken and half-ruined, and they had hoped for some habitation of living men, where there might be food to be had, for they had not eaten all that day. But the evening was darkening early, with rain in the wind, and any shelter was better than none. So they dismounted and stood their shields and lances against the outer wall, before unsaddling their horses and turning them loose to graze. Then they went into the chapel, and unbuckling and laying aside their swords, they knelt down before the age-worn altar, to make their evening prayers.

And when their prayers were done, hungry as they were, they lay down on the chancel floor to try to sleep.

But sleep they could not, for their empty bellies and the wind and rain outside. And as they lay half-wakeful in the darkest hour of the night, they saw a hand and a forearm clad in a sleeve of flame-red samite enter through the chapel door; and no man or woman whose arm it was but just the arm; and in the hand a tall candle, and hanging down from the wrist, a bridle, plainly and serviceably fashioned. And despite the wind that whistled through the crannies in the ancient walls, the candle burned bright and clear, straight-flamed as a laurel leaf, shedding its light all around.

The vision passed between them, and on up the chancel to the altar; and as suddenly as it had come, was gone again, leaving the chapel to the stormy dark.

And as they strained their eyes to make out what had become of it, they heard a voice, "Oh ye, weak in faith and dull in belief, these three things that ye have just now looked upon are the three things that ye lack. And for this reason ye ride up and down the forest ways and will never attain to the high adventure of the Holy Grail."

Then the voice was silent. And when the two knights,

awe-struck, had listened a while for it to come again, they turned towards each other in the dark. And Sir Gawain said, "Did you see what I saw?"

And Sir Ector said, "Did you hear what I heard?"

And both had seen, and both had heard, but neither could make any guess as to the meaning of the thing.

So they passed the rest of the night with little sleep; and in the morning when the storm had passed, saddled up and rode on, determined to seek a hermitage or an abbey where there might be some wise and holy man who could rede them the riddle.

But before ever they found such a place and such a man, they came out into a rich and open valley, and saw at a little distance a knight in full armour; but the sun was behind him, still low, and everything of a trembling dazzle after the night's rain, so that the device on his shield was dark to them.

As soon as he saw them, he shouted, "Joust!" in challenge, and turned his horse in their direction.

"Give me leave to take him first!" said Sir Ector.

But Sir Gawain was already galloping to meet his challenger. The clash of their meeting sent the birds bursting up from the woodshore, crying and calling in alarm; and both knights were lifted clean out of their saddles by the other's lance. But while Sir Gawain had taken no more harm than a dint to his shield, the other knight was speared right through the body, and the shaft snapped off as he fell, so that he lay transfixed, too sorely wounded to move.

Sir Gawain was on his feet before a man's heart might beat twice, and drawing his sword, called to the other to get up and fight if he would not lie there and be slain.

But the other answered, choking, "Alas, Sir Gawain, you have slain me already."

And when, with Sir Ector's help, Sir Gawain had unlaced and taken off the helm of the fallen man, he saw the white agonised face of Sir Owain the Bastard, who he had often jousted with in friendship at Camelot.

"Now curse the sun that flashed off your shields and hid the blazon," said Sir Owain. And then, "Here is an end, for me, of the Quest of the Holy Grail. Therefore take me to the abbey near here, that I may die among holy men and have Christian burial."

"There is no abbey in these parts, that I know of," said Sir Gawain; and the words strangled in his throat for the grief and horror that was upon him.

"Nay, but I passed by such a place, further down the valley," said Sir Owain. "Get me upon your horse, and I will guide you to it."

So Sir Gawain and Sir Ector lifted him up to the saddle, coughing blood when they moved him, and Sir Gawain mounted behind him to hold him from falling, while Sir Ector followed, leading Sir Owain's horse beside his own. And so, slowly and sorrowfully, they rode on until they came to the abbey. And there the monks gave them kind greeting, and Sir Owain was laid on the bed in the guest chamber.

And when he had prayed and made ready, he said with his last strength, "Now I am where I would be. When you go back to court, give my greeting to all of our brotherhood who you find there—though indeed it is in my heart that many will not return from this Quest—and bid them to remember me in their prayers. Now pull the lance-head from me, for I can bear this pain no longer."

So Sir Gawain, weeping, took hold of the broken lance-head, and quickly and strongly pulled it out from between his friend's ribs. And Sir Owain gave a groan and stretched himself all along, and the life went from him.

The monks brought a cloth of fine silk in which to wrap his body, and the funeral rites were performed, and he was buried in the abbey church.

Then Gawain and Ector would have ridden forward once more, though indeed the heart was gone out of them. But at the last moment, Sir Gawain bethought him of the vision that they had had in the deserted chapel, and that had been for the time driven from their minds. So he asked that they might speak with the father abbot. And while their horses waited in the outer courtyard, they stood before him in his chamber, and told him of what they had seen and heard, and asked him for the meaning.

The abbot was very old; and when Sir Gawain had done speaking, he sat for a long while with his chin sunk on his breast, so that they thought he dozed, and Sir Gawain began to fidget with his feet until the spurs jingled faintly on his heels. At last the father abbot looked up, and they saw that indeed he had not been dozing. "It is very simple. You saw a hand with a candle and a bridle, and a voice told you that these were the three things lacking in you. The hand is charity, and the vermilion sleeve is the Grace of God, which burns in charity with a constant flame, so that he that has it is filled with the love of Our Lord in Heaven. The bridle stands for self-control, for even as a man governs his horse with a bridle, so must he govern himself. The candle? The candle stands for truth, what else? The

truth of Christ. Lacking these three things, as the
told you, you will not attain to the adventure of
Holy Grail."

Then Sir Gawain grew very thoughtful, and sai
"Holy Father, if that is so, then it is useless for us t
continue this quest any further."

The old man bowed his head.

"So, sir," said Ector, heavily, "if we take your word
for it, it would be as well for us to turn about, and
return to Camelot."

"That is my advice. You will serve no purpose by
going on. No better purpose than you have served
already." And he gestured towards the little window in
the chamber wall, that looked down into the church
towards Sir Owain's grave.

But Sir Gawain and Sir Ector did not turn back, not
yet; for Sir Gawain was a stubborn man who did not
easily turn back at another's bidding from any path that
he had started out upon. And Sir Ector would not leave
his friend to go on alone.

And now the story leaves Sir Gawain, and tells again
of Sir Lancelot.

8

A HAIR SHIRT
AND AN UPHILL ROAD

Sir Lancelot remained with his holy man for three days; and at the end of that time a squire came riding out of the forest with a raking bay horse, and the helm and sword for which the priest had sent to ask of his brother. So next morning Sir Lancelot laced on the helm and belted the unfamiliar sword at his side, and thanking the priest for his goodness and asking him to pray for him, that he might not again fall into evil doing, he mounted the bay horse and rode on his way.

Towards noon he came upon a small chapel with a hermitage beside it. And drawing closer, he saw the black scar of a fire on the grass before the chapel, and an ancient man in a monk's white habit kneeling in the chapel doorway, beside the body of another who lay there dead. And the kneeling monk was crying out in grief and protest, "Dear God, why have you allowed this to be? He has served you heart and soul these many years, and could you not have kept him from this?"

Sir Lancelot dismounted and, hitching his horse's reins on a branch, came close and said, "God keep you, sir, you grieve most sorely for this man's death."

"Not for his death," said the aged monk, "but for the manner of it. For see the fine soft tunic that he wears, and his own garment cast aside."

And looking where the old man pointed, Lancelot saw a horrible hair-cloth shirt lying tumbled close to the dead feet. And still he did not understand.

"He was of my Order," said the monk, "though a fighting-man in his youth, and to us the wearing of fine linen is forbidden. Therefore, finding him like this, I know that the Devil must have come upon him at the last, and tempted him to the breaking of his vows, so that it was no godly death he died, and I cannot but fear that he is lost to all eternity."

And Sir Lancelot did not know what to answer, to comfort the old man.

But out of the sorrowful silence, another voice answered, quiet as a little wind through the treetops but clear as a trumpet call, "Nay, he is not lost, but most gloriously saved."

And looking round, Lancelot could see no one there; but clearly the old monk could see the speaker well enough, for he looked upward from his kneeling, as though at one standing tall above him; and wonder and the beginning of relief were on his face.

"Listen," said the voice, "and I will tell the manner of this man's death. Thou knowest that he was of noble birth, and still has kinsmen in these parts. Two days since, the Count of the Vale went to war with one of these kinsmen, Agoran by name. And the man who lies here, knowing his kinsfolk outnumbered and their cause just, took his sword from the place where he had laid it by, and turned fighting-man again on their behalf. So by the feats of valour that he performed, his kinsman had the victory; and the good man came back here to his hermitage to take up again his true life where he had laid it down.

"But followers of the Count knew at whose door to lay their defeat, and came after him, and called him out and would have cut him down with their swords. But though he was clad only in his habit and hair shirt, their blades turned and rebounded as though on the finest armour that was ever forged.

"This threw them into a mindless fury; and they fetched branches and lit a fire, saying they would see if the flames could do what their blades could not. And they stripped the old man to the skin, he making no resistance, but saying, 'If it be God's will that my time on earth is accomplished, then I shall die, and that will please me well. But if I die, it will be by God's will, and not the fire; for the fire has no power to burn a hair of my head; nor is there a garment in the world, whether it be my own hair shirt or of the finest linen ever woven, that would be so much as scorched, if I were to put it on now.'

"At this they cried 'Moonshine', with much laughter. And one of them tore off his own fine shirt, and they thrust it upon the old man in mockery, and cast him upon the flames.

"That was yester morning; and when they returned at night, the fire was newly burned out, and the old man lying there as peacefully as on a bed; and dead indeed, but with no mark nor scorch upon him when they dragged him from the hot ash; and the fine shirt upon him fresh and unmarked as thou seest it.

"Then great fear came upon them, and they ran, leaving him as thou didst find him here. Now therefore bury him in the white fine shirt, for it is no shame to him but the garment of his victory. And for the hair shirt he wore so many faithful years, there is another wearer waiting."

Then came a sudden gust of wind, and a dazzle of sunlight in and out between the swaying treetop branches; and when all was quiet again, the voice spoke no more.

And the old monk brought his gaze down to look at his dead friend in joy and relief.

He asked Sir Lancelot to bide with him in keeping watch beside the body, and help him next morning to bury it. So Sir Lancelot remained with him through the rest of that day. And again he made his confession, and the old monk gave him much good advice. And next day, when they had buried the holy man before the altar of his little chapel, and the knight was making ready to arm and ride away, the monk said to him, "Sir Lancelot, last night, when I had heard your confession, I gave you absolution and blessing. Now, before you ride on, I give you your penance. It is that you shall wear this hair shirt from now on. And further, I charge you to eat no meat and drink no wine while you follow the quest on which you have started out. But above all, keep to the hair shirt, for while you wear it it shall keep you from further sin."

So Sir Lancelot stripped, and took up the hair shirt of the man he had just helped to bury, and pulled it on, with its rasping bristles next to his bare skin, and then put on his tunic and then his harness. And so he took his leave of the old monk, and mounted and rode away.

That night he came to a woodland shrine where two ways parted, and laid him down there with his shield for a pillow. Watching and fasting had wearied him out, till not even the prickling and chafing of the hair shirt could keep him awake. But his sleep was restless and broken with dreams, and with the first cobweb light of dawn he was glad to be up and riding on.

Noon found him in a valley between wooded cliffs, all shut in and murmurous with small winged things among the young bracken. And there riding towards him he beheld the knight who had robbed him of horse and helm and his well-loved sword Joyeux before the chapel of the Grail.

The knight saw him in the same instant, and shouted to him to defend himself or he was a dead man, then struck spurs to his horse—Lancelot's horse—and rode at him full tilt. Sir Lancelot spurred to meet him, anger and gladness mingled in his answering shout. The point of the other knight's lance took him in the shoulder; but though it broke through the links of his hauberk it did little more than gash the skin, and he crouched low in the saddle, and gathering up all his strength, got in a blow that brought the horse crashing down and all but lifted the rider's head from his shoulders, as he galloped past. Without pause, he wrenched round and came thundering back on his tracks; but although the horse was already struggling up, the knight lay where he had fallen among the bracken, and the fight was over.

Then Sir Lancelot dismounted and took Joyeux from the fallen man's sheath, leaving the blade that he himself had carried since yesterday in its place. The battered helmet was not worth the taking back. He tied the bay to a birch tree where the knight would find it when he came to himself and was fit to ride, and took back his own horse, that came at his whistle and was dear to him like his sword—it had been a bad moment when he saw the horse go down—and rode on.

And as he rode, his heart lightened and warmed within him, and the prickling and chafing of his hair shirt where his armour pressed it against his skin was a kind of sharp joy to him, for he thought that the winning back of his horse and his sword was maybe a sign that God's face was no longer quite turned away from him, and the strength and potency of his knighthood were given back to him once more.

Sir Lancelot rode for many days in the forest and along the fringes of the Waste Land, sleeping now beneath the roof of a holy man or a forester or a hurdle maker, now under a tree or at the foot of a wayside cross, or on open heathland, where the night wind searched him to the bone. He dreamed strange dreams in his solitude as he slept by night and rode by day, of men with stars between their eyes, and trees that bore bright and bitter fruit, and knights who turned into lions, and lions who grew sky-wide wings. And still he looked and listened for tidings of the knight with the red cross on the white shield. For he knew in his heart that that knight had some special meaning for him. And always he looked and listened for tidings of Sir Galahad, not knowing that they were one and the same. And always he rode with his heart wide open, waiting for God to tell him what next to do in the following of his quest.

One day he came out into a vast clearing in the forest, and saw in the midst of it a strong and splendid castle. Between him and the castle lay a wide meadow; and clustered all round the meadow verges, bright as the small flowers of spring time, were tents and pavilions, striped and chequered, blue and violet, green, red and yellow, each blinking with goldwork on fluttering pennants. And in the open midst of the meadow a great tournament was going forward.

Five hundred knights at least, he judged, were taking part; and half of them were cloaked and armed in black as glossy midnight-deep as ravens' feathers, while the other half were cloaked and armed in white; the proud fierce white of swan's wing or lightning flash. And the white knights had taken up the side towards the castle, while the black had the side towards the forest, so that their backs were to Sir Lancelot as he sat his horse and watched them.

And as he watched, it seemed to him that the raven ranks were getting the worst of the contest. He saw that they were beginning to fall back towards him; and his lance hand itched and his knees tightened their grip on his horse's flanks, and instantly he was on their side, as he had always been on the side of anyone hard pressed by a stronger man. And next moment, scarce knowing what he did, he had struck in his spurs and, couching his lance, was out from the woodshore to their aid.

He took the first knight to come against him with such force that he brought down both horse and rider; the next he got with the point to the helmet-crest, the most difficult stroke of all and only to be attempted by a master. Then thundering on, he broke his lance against a third man's shield, yet unhorsed him all the same; and drawing his sword, plunged on into the thick of the struggle. And there he fought so valiantly, dealing out such skilled and mighty blows, that he should surely have carried off the crown of any tournament. Yet it seemed that not all his strength and skill and valour could avail against the ranks of the white champions. His blows might have landed upon mighty tree trunks, or Joyeux have been no more than a sword of plaited rushes, for all the harm he seemed able to do the men he fought with, and he was powerless to check their forward thrust that drove the black knights back and back.

Again and again he charged them, striving to break an opening in their ranks, again and again he failed, until he could barely lift his sword arm for weariness, and though there was no scathe on him, his whole body was drained of strength as a man sore wounded may be drained of his life's blood.

At last a band of the white knights surrounded him and bore him down by main force, and dragged him off into the forest; while without his aid the raven ranks were quickly overwhelmed and put to flight.

Once in the forest, Sir Lancelot looked for death and did not care; but his captors simply turned him free, and that was the worst shame of all.

"Let you remember," said one of the white knights, "that though it comes about by our strength and not by your choosing, you are of our company now. Remember that, and ride on your way."

One of them gave him his sword again, and he sheathed it, fumblingly, at his side. And, slumped wearily in the saddle, his head on his breast, he rode away.

Never before, no matter how long or hard the fighting, had this dreadful weakness sapped his sword arm; never before had he been taken prisoner in a tournament, never before had he been captured and then turned free in casual mercy. And what was left of his pride was bleeding-raw within him. "Now," he thought, "I have lost everything; my love, and the strength of my knighthood; and God's face is still turned away from me."

That night he passed in a wild and craggy place far from the haunts of men, dividing the dark hours between little sleep and much prayer. And in the morning, when the sky was clear-washed with light in the east, and the birds began to sing, he prayed again; and as he prayed, and the sun rose and dazzled into his eyes, a new feeling came upon him. Not hope, quieter than hope, but a kind of peace, an acceptance that what had happened to him yesterday, whatever happened to him henceforth, it was God's will for him; even if it was God's will that he should remain shut out.

And he saddled his horse again and rode on.

He came at last to a valley running down between sides of sheer black rock, to a mighty river. And on the bank of the river, mounted on a great warhorse of his own colour, waited a knight in armour so black that the blackness had a bloom on it like the bloom on a thundercloud, and cast its own darkness over the daylight all around. At sight of Sir Lancelot he struck in his spurs and came for him full tilt, at such speed that there was no chance of avoiding him, nor of getting in the first thrust. His levelled lance took Sir Lancelot's horse in the breast, so that it screamed and reared up, then came crashing down with its scarlet heart's blood fountaining from the wound. And the black rider on his black steed whirled on unchecked, and in a few breaths of time was lost to sight.

Sir Lancelot scrambled to his feet, and stood looking down at his dead horse; and grief was heavy in him, for they were old friends and had been through many adventures together. But for himself, he cared nothing that he had been worsted yet again. All that was over with him. He accepted it as the will of God, and unslung his shield from the saddle-bow, and started walking towards the river.

When he reached it, he saw how wide and deep and fast it ran, so that there could be no way over without a boat or wings. The rocky bluffs on either side of the valley were beyond any man's scaling, and to turn back into the forest would be a backward-going over the way he had come. So he laid aside helm and shield, and lay down in the lee of a mossy outcrop of the rocks on the river bank, for the daylight was fading fast, to wait until God should show him the way forward.

And so he fell into the deepest and quietest sleep that he had known for many a long night.

And now the story leaves Sir Lancelot and tells again of Sir Bors.

9

SIR BORS
MAKES A HARD CHOICE

For many days after he left the lady of the tower Sir Bors wandered, while the forest darkened to full summer about him.

And one warm heavy noontide he came to a place where two tracks crossed each other. And as he checked there, wondering which to take, he heard the sound of horses' hooves; and looking in that direction, he saw riding hard towards him two hedge-knights, and between them his own brother, Lional, stripped to his breeks, and with his hands bound before him. One of the knights was dragging his horse by its shortened rein, and the other had a long spiny thorn branch in his hand, with which he was viciously lashing their captive as they went.

Bors was just about to dash to the rescue when the hoof-drum of another horse ridden at full gallop came upon him from the other side, and with it the sound of a woman screaming. And snatching a desperate glance that way, he saw a knight riding furiously across the open glade, with a maiden across his saddle-bow, who fought and screamed in the grip of his bridle-arm, her long fair hair flying over his shoulder like a banner of pale silk.

Seeing Sir Bors, she screamed more loudly yet, and held imploring arms to him as the horse plunged on into the trees. And, the hedge-knights drawing near, he saw his brother's face turned to him in wild hope as he was dragged past, and as they turned down the middle track, his brother's back, crimson-striped from neck to waist, and the blood oozing out between each stroke of the thorn branch.

The choice must be made, and on the instant, and the making of it felt like something within him being torn in two.

He flung a hurried prayer heavenward, "Lord Jesus Christ, protect my brother for me until I can come back to his aid!" And before the prayer had flown, he was away full gallop after the knight and the maiden.

It was not long before he had them again in sight, and shouted after them, "Sir knight, set the maiden down, or you are a dead man!"

At that, the knight checked, and slipped the maiden from his saddle-bow; but then hitched round his shield and drawing his sword made straight for Sir Bors with a bellow of fury. But Sir Bors was ready for him, and beat up his blade, then slipped his point in under the shield and took him below the breast, bursting through his hauberk and the body-flesh beneath, so that he flung up his arms and pitched from the saddle, and was a dead man before he hit the ground.

Then Sir Bors went to the maiden, who was standing white-faced nearby. "Damsel, you are safe now from this knight. What more would you have me do?"

"Accept my thanks," said the maiden, "and take me home—oh, pray you take me home; it is not far from here."

Everything in Bors was crying out to be away back to his brother; but he could not leave the maiden alone in the forest; so he fetched the dead knight's horse and mounted her on it, then remounted himself, and led the way in the direction that she bade him.

They had not gone far when they met with twelve knights, who set up a joyful shout and came spurring towards them. But when Sir Bors would have drawn his sword again, she stayed him, saying, "These are of my father's household. They will have been out scouring the forest for me."

Then there was a joyful coming together; and the maiden and the knights would all have had Sir Bors return with them to her father's castle. But Sir Bors shook his head. "Gladly I would come; but I have sore need to be elsewhere, and that as quickly as may be!"

And seeing in his face that the matter was indeed desperate, they pressed him no further, but bade him God speed. And so he left them and headed back as fast as his horse could carry him, to the place where he had abandoned his brother, and on down the track that the hedge-knights had taken.

He had followed it but a short way, when he came upon a tall man with face half-hidden by a monk's dark cowl, standing beside the way, and reined in to ask if he had seen them pass.

"Look for yourself," said the monk, "and see that which was your brother when you left him." And he pointed down into the wayside tangle of fern and brambles. And looking where he pointed, Sir Bors saw, as it seemed, the body of his brother Lional, with the blood still fresh upon it, lying there like a broken toy that some careless child had thrown aside.

Grief broke over Bors in a wave, and he dropped from his horse, and kneeling, cradled the body in his arms. And within himself he cried out, "Lord Jesus, I prayed to you to guard him, and you did not heed! You did not heed!" But he thrust the desperate protest aside, and said, "Oh God, thy will be done," and lifted the body, feeling it almost weightless in his arms, and laid it across his saddle. And to the monk standing by, he said, "Good sir, is there a church or chapel near here, where I can bury my brother?"

"There is," said the monk. "Do you follow me, and I will lead you there."

And so, leading his horse, Sir Bors followed where the cowled figure led.

Presently they came to a tall, strong-set tower rising

among the trees as though it too were rooted there rather than built by the labour of men, and close beside it a moss-grown and deserted chapel. Before the chapel door they checked, and Sir Bors lifted down the body of his brother, and carrying it within, looked about for some fitting place to lay it down. The light in the chapel was dim and green, and showed him in the centre of the place a great flat-topped tomb of carved stone. And there, since there seemed nowhere else, he laid the body.

But search how he would, he could find neither cross nor candles nor any sign of Christian usage in that place.

"It grows late. Leave him here," said the monk. "Spend the dark hours yonder in the tower; and in the morning, come back with me, and we will bury him as befits a knight."

So with a heavy heart, Sir Bors left the strange chapel, and followed the monk into the tower hard by.

Now from the outside, the tower had seemed as forsaken to the hoot-owl as the chapel beside it; but as he crossed the threshold he was met by the glow of torches and the music of minstrels, and surrounded by many knights and ladies in gay silken garments, who made him welcome and brought him into the Great Hall and helped him to unarm, and gave him a robe, gold-diapered and lined with the softest marten skins, to cover his shirt.

Then a lady came into the Hall, more beautiful and gracious than any woman that ever he had seen before, with eyes as softly and deeply blue as nightshade flowers, and hair that shone red-gold through the purple silken web that bound it up. She came to Bors, and bade him welcome also, for clearly she was the mistress of the strange stronghold; and led him to sit beside her on a cushioned bench, while the pages and squires made the long tables ready for supper. And she asked him how he came to be there; and he told her of his quest, and of his brother's death, at which she made soft sounds of grief for his grief, and would have taken his hand where it lay upon his knee, but that slowly, and careful to do her no discourtesy, he drew it away.

When he did this, she started and trembled, and asked him, "Bors, am I ugly to you?"

"No, lady," said Bors, "you are among the fairest that ever I saw."

At that she sighed, and smiled a little. "Then let you prove it to me. For so long—since first I heard account of you at Arthur's court, I have held you in my heart and waited for your coming. So long, I have waited, refusing others who might have made me happy, for your sake. And now—will you not love me in return?"

At this Bors was silent, not knowing what to say. And in a little the lady said, "I can give you power, greater riches than any man has ever had before you." And that made it a little easier for Bors to hold out against her beauty and the soft light in her eyes.

"Ah, lady," he said, "I have told you of the quest on which I ride, and that my brother, whom I loved better than anyone else in the world, lies newly dead in the chapel at your gates, I know not how or why. I am not free to love any lady."

"Forget the quest," said she, "I can give you greater joy. Your brother is dead, and grieving will not bring him back." And she leaned forward, holding out her hands. "It is not easy for a woman to beg a man for his love, but I lay down my pride and beg for yours, for I love you as never a woman loved a man before."

"Lady," said Sir Bors, "I would do anything else to make you happy, but this I cannot do."

Then she began to weep, and rock herself to and fro like a woman keening for her dead, and pull down her bright hair all about her. And Sir Bors, suddenly weary, got up to go and seek his armour, that he might return to the chapel.

When she saw that none of this could move him, she cried out to him, "You are cruel and heartless! A false knight; for you have brought me to such grief and shame that I will kill myself before your eyes, rather than live another hour to suffer so!"

And she bade her knights lay hold of him and bring him out to the courtyard and safe-keep him there. And she called twelve maidens from among those in the Hall; and bidding them follow her she climbed the outside stair to the highest rampart. And when they stood there between the torchlight and the moon, one of the maidens called down into the courtyard, "Sir Bors, oh, Sir Bors, if you are a true knight, have pity on us now, and grant my lady what she begs; for if she jumps from this tower for love of you, we must assuredly jump with her, for we are hers, and cannot let her die alone!"

Bors, standing pinioned, looked up at them, seeing how fair they were, and how young, and pity tore at him; and he shouted back at them in a fury, "If your lady jumps, and if you jump with her, that is for you to choose. I cannot and I will not love her."

At that, with wild lamentations, they all sprang out into the empty air, and fell like so many bright birds brought down by the fowler's arrow.

And Sir Bors tore himself free, and in the horror of

that moment, crossed himself.

In the instant that he did so, he seemed to be engulfed in a great cloud of stinking darkness shot through with murky flame, and a great shrieking and howling as though all the fiends of Hell whirled about him. He was beaten to his knees, deafened and dizzy as it seemed the whole castle turned upside down. And when, little by little, the cloud and the tumult cleared, and he shook his head and looked about him, the tower and the lady and the knights and maidens were all gone. Only his armour lay scattered in the moonlight on the sour grass before him, and his horse grazed undisturbed nearby; and he was crouching beside the doorway to the deserted chapel.

Still on his knees, he thanked God for his deliverance, then, getting to his feet, stumbled inside.

But there was no body lying on the ancient stone tomb, no sign of his brother anywhere; and it came to him that what he had thought was Lional's body must have been, like all else of that night's adventure, part of a snare laid for him by the Lord of Darkness.

All might yet be well with Lional, and his heart lightened with a gleam of hope; and it being by then near to dawn, he armed himself, and whistled up and saddled his horse, and set out once more along the forest ways, hoping that somewhere ahead he might get word of his brother.

Two days later he came to yet another castle; and close before it he met with a young squire, and checked to ask him if there was any news worth the telling and hearing.

"Indeed yes," said the boy, "tomorrow there is to be

a most splendid tournament here, between our own knights and those who follow the Count of the Plain."

Hearing this, Sir Bors determined to stay until the morrow. It might well be that other knights of the Grail Quest would gather to such a tournament, and from someone among them he might get word of his brother. Maybe Lional would even come himself. For he had begun to hope that his sight of Lional captive and beaten was as unreal as the rest of the night's adventure that had followed it.

So, thanking the squire, he made on towards a hermitage which he could just see far off on the forest verge, hoping to beg shelter there for the night.

As he drew nearer, he saw a horse that he thought he recognised grazing under the trees, and pushed forward with a quickened heart. And when he reached the hermitage, there, sitting in the doorway, was no holy man, but Lional himself, surrounded by his armour and polishing away at his sword against tomorrow's tournament. Lional looked up as he drew near, but when he saw who it was, his face set like a stone. And as Bors flung himself from his horse to greet him with joy, he made no move, but only rubbed the harder at the sword blade across his knee.

"Lional!" cried Bors. "Oh, my brother, how is it with you?"

"It is no thanks to you, that it is not death with me," said Lional between his teeth, "as it would have been, but that a flash of forked lightning came out of a clear sky, and killed those two who had me in their power; and that left to myself I was able to burst free of my bonds." He rubbed the red rope-burns on his wrists as he spoke. But his eyes never left Bors's face. "I would have died for you, Bors, and you left me in sorest peril of my life to go to the rescue of a maiden who was nothing to you."

To Bors, it was as though his brother had struck him. He knelt down before him with bowed head and joined hands, "God knows I did what I thought was right. Lional, pray you forgive me."

Lional stumbled to his feet and began to gather up his armour without a word.

"What are you doing?" Bors said, still kneeling.

"Getting myself armed, as you see. I was a fool to think I had a brother to love and trust; but even I am not such a fool as to think that I can fight you in nothing but my shirt, while you are fully armed."

"Lional, in God's name, no!" Bors said, watching.

"There is only one way to stop me from killing you," Lional said, "and that is for you to kill me."

"No!" Bors said again. "You are my brother!"

"I *was* your brother." Lional fastened the last buckle. He was beside himself with grief and rage. He mounted his horse and wrenched it round towards where Bors still knelt as though frozen. "Get up!" he yelled. "Get on your horse and fight me. If you do not, I swear I'll kill you kneeling there, and put up with the shame that will follow me afterwards."

Bors tried once more, stretching out his hands, humbling himself as he had never humbled himself to any man before. "Lional, have pity on us both, remembering the love between us; and do not kill me kneeling here, for I cannot and I will not fight you."

Lional let out a harsh cry, and struck his horse so that it plunged forward, hurling Bors over backwards and trampling him under the great round hooves; and as he lay groaning and half-conscious on the ground, hurled himself from the saddle and began to drag and wrench at his brother's helmet like a madman, his sword ready in his other hand.

But at that moment, the hermit, who had heard all that passed, yet waited, hoping that they might heal the quarrel for themselves, came hobbling out from his bothie, and seeing Lional about to hack off his brother's head, flung himself down over the injured knight, crying out, "For God's sake hold your hand! Would you kill your brother, and your own soul with him?"

"Get out of my way, old man," said Lional, "or I shall kill you first and him after, and my soul may pay for both!"

But the hermit only clung to Bors the closer, gripping his shoulders and shielding his body with his own.

And so Lional killed him lying there, with one sword stroke that split his skull under the thin silvery hair; and heaving the old man's body aside, went back to work on his brother's helmet.

But it so chanced that at that very moment another knight of the Round Table, Sir Colgrevance by name, who had also heard of tomorrow's tournament, came riding up, and saw what went forward. And he flung himself from the saddle, and seizing Lional by the shoulders, heaved him backwards, shouting, "Lional! Are you mad? Would you kill your brother?"

"Yes," said Lional, struggling free, "but if you meddle in the matter, I shall kill you first, as I did the old man."

"Then I fear that you must try it," said Sir Colgrevance, getting between Lional and his brother, and drawing his sword and hitching his shield from behind his shoulder.

The fight between them was fierce and deadly, for both were mighty champions, and had been matched in friendly combat so often that they knew each other's swordplay as well as they did their own. And it went on so long that Bors began to come back to himself. He dragged up on to one elbow, and saw the dead hermit lying close by, and his brother and his friend in desperate combat; and horror rose in him, and he struggled to get to his feet and come between them. He managed to sit up, but the world swam round him, and for pain and weakness he could get no further.

And the fight was beginning to go against Sir Colgrevance, and seeing Sir Bors sitting up, he shouted to him, "Come and help me, man! It is for you I fight; and if I die, it will be on you the shame!"

At this, Bors managed to get his legs under him, and half stood up. And all the while Sir Colgrevance was panting and sobbing out to him for help; but before he could take a step towards the battling figures, Sir Lional got in one last great blow that split his opponent's helm and bit deep into his head, so that he gave a great choking cry and went down sprawling into death.

Then Lional turned on his brother, and dealt him a blow that sent him half down again. "Fight!" he shouted, "Fight, or die like the faithless coward you are!"

Bors drew his sword. The tears were running down his face, but he drew his sword and found his shield. The world was steadying under him, and the strength coming back into his arm. "God forgive me," he prayed. "Sweet Lord Jesus Christ, forgive me!" And he raised his sword . . .

Something happened between his shield and Lional's,

as when the sun flashes off polished metal, but a thousand times brighter; there was a crack as of thunder, and a blast of searing heat, and they were flung back from each other and hurled half-stunned to the ground.

And when, in a little, their eyes cleared and their senses returned to them, they saw the ground between them blackened as by fire, and their shields twisted and scorched. Yet neither of them had taken any harm at all, save the wounds that had been on them already.

Then a great quiet came upon them; and out of the quiet, Bors heard a voice which said to him, "Bors, get up now, and leave this place. The time has come that you must part from your brother, and make your way to the sea, where Percival waits for you."

Then Bors went to his brother, and they put their arms round each other. "Lional, my most dear brother," he said, "do you bide here, and see that these two who died for my sake are laid in the ground with all the honour that is due to them."

"I will do that," said Lional. "But you? Will you not stay too?"

Bors shook his head. "I am to go to the sea, where Percival waits for me. But I think that when all is over, we shall see each other again."

So they parted.

And by and by, when all was done for Sir Colgrevance and the holy man, Sir Lional went back to Arthur's court, for his heart was not in the Quest any more.

But Sir Bors rode away, down to the sea.

He rode day and night until he came to an abbey on the coast; and there he lodged one night. And as he slept, the voice came to him again: "Arise, Bors, and go down now to the shore."

So he rose and armed himself, and saddled his horse and brought it from the stable, and rode down towards the sound of the sea in his ears.

When he came to the shore, he found a ship lying close into the rocks, seemingly empty, and set with sails of white samite, so that she was like no ship he had ever seen before. He dismounted and went on board, and instantly, before he could embark his horse as he had meant to do, she drew away from the shore, and the wind filled her sails and sent her speeding like a seabird over the waves. He looked round him, but the night was too dark to make out any details of the vessel; and since there seemed nothing else to be done, he took off his battered helm, and, commending himself to God, lay down in a sheltered corner and went to sleep.

The first thing he saw when he woke in the morning was the yellow head of Sir Percival as he sat rubbing his eyes in the early sun.

Percival saw him in the same moment, and they cried out each other's names and stumbled towards each other with joyful greetings. "How do you come to be here?" Percival asked. "For I was alone in this ship, as I have been for many days, when I fell asleep last evening."

And they exchanged news of all that had happened to them since they were last together.

"Now we need only Galahad to join us," said Percival, "for the promise that was made to me to be altogether fulfilled."

But now the story leaves Bors, and tells again of that same Galahad.

10

THE SHIP AND THE SWORD

Now the story runs that when Sir Galahad had left Sir Percival after saving him from the twenty knights, he took his way through the Waste Forest, and there met with many adventures.

And so he came, on a day, to the abbey where Sir Percival had seen King Mordrain lying; he that had first owned the white shield with the blood-red cross. And he heard King Mordrain's story; how that he had waited in wounds and blindness so many years, for the shield's next master to set him free.

So next morning he went at the time of Mass to the abbey church where the King lay.

And when Mass was over, he drew near, the iron grille opening to let him through. And King Mordrain rose on his bed and held out gaunt arms to him; and the light came back into his eyes, so that he saw him clear.

"Long has been the waiting time," said Mordrain, with great gladness. "But now it comes to its end."

And Galahad caught him as he swayed, and sat down at the head of the bed and laid him back against his shoulder. And suddenly in that moment the old wounds were healed over, leaving not even their scars behind.

"Now I have all that my heart longed for," said the King. "Now, Lord God, let me come to you in peace, for my sorrows are over."

And lying against Galahad's shoulder, he gave a long, slow, contented sigh, and his spirit went free.

And when he had been buried as befitted a king, Sir Galahad rode on his way, for he knew that the time had come for him to ride towards the sea.

But as he headed for the coast, he came one shimmering late summer noontide to a place where a great tournament was going forward. Indeed it was almost over, for those knights whom he judged to be defending their castle, were outnumbered and outmatched and beginning to be driven back.

Galahad drew his sword and spurred forward to their aid. And he performed such mighty feats of championship, and hurled so many of the attackers from their saddles, that the defenders took heart and began to press forward again, as though the Archangel Michael himself had come among them.

Now Sir Gawain and Sir Ector, who had also chanced

upon the tournament and were fighting on the other side, saw the white shield with the red cross blazing in the midst of the *mêlée*; and by now most of the Quest knights knew whose device that was, and they began to think that maybe they would withdraw from the struggle and look for an adventure elsewhere. But before they could do so, by the chance of battle, Sir Galahad came straight that way, and in the close fighting, dealt Sir Gawain such a blow on the head that his sword bit through helm and mail-coif and brought him crashing to the ground.

Then he swept on, and was lost in the roaring swirl of men and horses. And the fighting had turned as a tide turns and began to shift away from the castle, while Sir Ector got his horse head-on to the flood and managed to hold him there, guarding his fallen friend and keeping him from being trampled as he lay on the ground.

The attacking knights broke and streamed away; with the defenders hot in pursuit. But presently the knights of the castle came back from their hunting, and found Sir Ector kneeling over his friend; and they gathered Sir Gawain up with the rest of the wounded, and bore him back to the castle, and sent for a physician to salve and bind his head. Then Sir Gawain opened his eyes and said, "My head is sore hurt—and I am like to die."

"In a month you will be fit to ride and carry arms again," said the physician.

Then Sir Gawain said to Sir Ector, "Now, if you are for riding on, you must ride on without me, for as soon as I can ride indeed, I am away back to Camelot. This looked to be a fine quest at the outset, but it has brought me nothing but sorrow and a sore head." And then he added, as though that made it worse, "There is no standing against *that one*. I am thinking that if I had got my blow in first, he would not have bled at all!"

"Somehow, I would scarce expect him to," said Sir Ector, in a puzzled voice.

"Any more than one would expect it of a stone or a flame or a lily, or St Michael himself," said Sir Gawain, with disgust. "I had sooner the men I fight or ride with were flesh and blood!"

So in a few days they parted, and Sir Ector rode on alone.

Sir Galahad had not returned with the castle knights. When they looked for him at their turning back from the pursuit, he was simply not there. He had ridden on towards the sea.

He rode so far and fast that dusk of that same day found him not two leagues from Corbenic. But he knew within himself that for him the Quest was not yet ready to be accomplished, nor his journeying to the Grail Castle done. And so, passing a hermitage by the way, he stopped there to ask shelter for the night. And the hermit fed him and gave him a spread of fresh grass to sleep on.

But in the dark hour of the night there came the nearing sound of horse's hooves, and a light quick beating on the door, and a woman's voice calling for Sir Galahad.

And Sir Galahad rose and went to the door, and found there a maiden, holding the bridle of a little palfrey.

"What is it that you would with me?" he asked.

"Arm yourself, and mount and follow me; and I will

lead you to the highest adventure that ever a knight beheld."

So Galahad went back into the hermitage and armed himself while the maiden caught and saddled his horse that grazed nearby. And he took his leave of the hermit, and mounted, and went with her.

They were far on their way when the sun rose and dusty-gilded the dark spreading trees of late summer. And all that day and far into the night, they rode, not stopping to eat or rest. And in the clear green half-dark of the next dawn, they began to hear the sounding of the sea. So they came down to the shore, and found there waiting for them a ship whose drooping sails were all of white samite, and Bors and Percival standing on the deck, looking for them to come.

"We must turn our horses loose here," said the maiden, and slipped to the ground, lifting down after her a casket of rare and exquisitely carved wood, which she had carried on her saddle-bow all the way. Sir Galahad dismounted also, and unsaddled both horses and turned them loose to graze. Then he went down to the vessel, and stepped aboard, helping the maiden, still with her beautiful carved casket, over the side after him. Then there were great rejoicings, as the companions greeted each other; and for Sir Percival especially, when he saw the maiden, and knew her for his sister Anchoret, whom he had not seen for many years. And a great joy and peace of heart rose in all of them, at their coming together again.

And a wind came out of the quiet dawn and filled the sails, so that when the sun rose clear of the world's edge they were far out to sea, beyond sight of any land. And still the three knights were talking; sometimes gravely, sometimes with laughter, telling each other of all that had passed since last they were together. But at last, when the sun had risen high enough to glow like a blurred golden rose through the white samite curve of the sail, a little silence fell between them. And Sir Bors said, "Now it seems to me that if my lord Lancelot, your father, were here, there would be nothing more that we could wish for, save for the fair ending of our quest."

"To me also," said Sir Galahad. "But it is not God's will."

All that day and all the next night the ship sped before the wind; and at dayspring they came to a low rocky island alive with the crying and calling of sea birds. And as though there was an unseen hand at the steering-oar, they headed up a narrow hidden creek; and the wind fell from the sails and the ship settled to rest. And just ahead of them beyond a sandy spur of the shore, so that she could only be reached on foot, they saw another ship much richer and larger than their own.

"Good sirs," said the maiden Anchoret, who had kept herself happily apart, and scarcely spoken since the joyful moment of greeting her brother, "yonder is the adventure for which Our Lord has gathered you together. Do you come now, and see."

So they sprang ashore, helping her among them, and she still carrying the beautiful casket cradled in her arms, and went scrambling across the dunes to the strange ship. When they got there, they saw written on her side: "Oh man who would set foot in me, take heed that thou be full of faith. For I am Faith, and if thou fail me, I shall fail thee."

Then Bors and Percival hesitated on the shore. But

Galahad stepped aboard, and the maiden with him, and so the other two followed.

In the midst of the ship, under an airy canopy, they found a bed spread with fair silks and linens. And at the head of the bed rested a golden crown, and across the foot lay the most beautiful sword that any of them had ever seen; with a handspan of its blade drawn from the sheath. And the pommel was of one great gem-stone that shone with all the colours under Heaven; and engraved on the quillions were the words, "None was ever able to grip me, none ever shall, save one alone; and he shall surpass all who came before him, and all who come after."

"Here is a marvellous claim!" said Sir Percival. "Let us test its truth." And he reached out to take up the sword. But big as he was, his hand could not encircle the grip. Then Sir Bors tried, with no better success. And then they looked to Sir Galahad. But he said, "Not yet." He was reading some words wonderfully etched on the unsheathed part of the blade. "Let no man draw me from my scabbard, unless he can outdo and outdare every other. Death it is to any lesser man who draws me."

"Why has the sword been left half-drawn from its sheath?" said Sir Bors at last, as they stood looking down at it. "It is not good for a blade to be left exposed so, especially in the sea air."

"I can tell you that story," said the maiden Anchoret. "Long ago, when King Pelles, who men call the Maimed King, was whole and strong, he rode out hunting one day in his forest that stretches along the sea. He became separated from his hounds and huntsmen, and all his knights save one, and trying to find his way back to them, he came at last through the forest to the coast which faces Ireland. And there, lying in a deep inlet, he found this ship on which we now stand. He read the words upon the side, but he was as good as any earthly knight; he had faith in God, as strong as any other, and he knew of no sin that he had committed against his God. And so he boarded the ship, while the knight who was with him waited on the shore. He found the sword, and unsheathed it by as much as you can see; but before he could draw it completely from the sheath, there came a spear flying out of nowhere, and pierced him through the thigh, making a wound which has never healed but maims him to this day. And in the moment of his wounding, his land was wounded also, and became as it is now; a land in which the waters do not flow and the harvest fails, and trees grow stunted and men and cattle hollow-eyed. And so it must remain until the man who draws this sword shall heal the King of his wound."

And still they looked down upon the half-drawn sword; and as they looked, they saw another strange thing: that the sheath was worthy of the wondrous smith-craft it contained, of some strange skin the colour of a red rose and wrought over with gold and blue, but where there should have been a rich sword belt for its support, there was nothing but a length of hempen rope, so poor and frayed that it would surely not support the weight of its weapon for an hour without breaking. And on the scabbard, in letters twisted among the blue and the gold so that they made part of the enrichment, they read, "Let not any man take off this sword belt to replace it with a better. That is for a maiden's doing, and one that is without sin and the daughter of a king and a queen. And she shall replace it with another, made from that about herself which is most precious to her."

Then the three knights fell to wondering how they were to find the right maiden. And listening to them, Anchoret smiled, and said, "Sirs, do not lose heart. So it please God, the new belt shall be in its place before we leave this ship. As rich and beautiful and potent a belt as even such a sword as this demands."

And as they all turned to look at her, she opened the casket that she had carried all that while, and drew out a belt woven of gold thread and silk and strands of yellow hair; and the hair so bright and burnished that it was hard to tell it from the threads of gold; and brilliant gems strung among the fantastic braids, and gold buckles to make all secure.

"Good sirs," said she, "I am the daughter of a king and of a queen, as my brother Percival knows. And I have never knowingly sinned; and this sword belt I braided of the most precious thing I had, my hair. Last Pentecost a voice spoke to me, telling of what was before me, and what I must do; and I obeyed the voice, and cut off my hair, which maybe I loved too much; but I cut it gladly, none the less, and wrought with it as you see."

And while they watched, finding no words to speak, she bent over the sword and untied the hempen rope, and fitted on the beautiful belt as skilfully as though it had been her daily task.

"Now," said Bors, drawing a long breath when it was done, and turning to Galahad, "put on your sword."

And Percival echoed him, "Put on your sword."

"First I must make sure of my right to it," said Galahad. And he took it by the hilt, and his hand closed

round the grip with the ease of familiar things, as though
it were a sword of his own, long lost, and found again.
And as his watching companions caught their breaths,
he unsheathed it and let the light play on the blade,
smiling a little. Then he slid it back into the sheath; and
the maiden unbuckled his old sword, the sword that
he had drawn from its red marble block in the river
below Camelot, and laid it in the place left empty across
the foot of the bed, and buckled on the new one.

"This is your sword," she said. "It has been waiting
for you since the world stood at morning."

"For your part in this," said Galahad, looking down
at her, where her veil had fallen back from her bright
boy's head, "I cannot speak my thanks. I would that
you were my sister, as you are Percival's. But sister or
no, I am your true knight, for ever."

11

DEATH OF A MAIDEN

So the three knights and the maiden returned to their
own ship; and as soon as they were on board the wind
caught and filled the sail and carried them swiftly from
the islet.

More days passed; and one morning the ship came
sailing into a small land-locked harbour far to the north
of any lands that they had known before. And since it
seemed to them that their ship would not have brought
them so surely to this landfall, if it were not for some
purpose, they went ashore and took the track which ran
up from the waterside and looked as though it must lead
to some living-place of men.

Presently the track lifted over a moorland ridge, and

they saw before them the dark mass of a castle rising like a rock-crag from the heather that washed to its walls. And as they stood looking, ten knights came riding out through the castle gateway; and behind them a maiden carrying a great silver bowl.

When they came up, the leader of the troop spoke to Sir Galahad, with no courtesy of greeting. "The maiden you have with you is of noble birth?"

"She is the daughter of a king and of a queen," said Sir Galahad.

"Has she ever sinned?"

"Never. That is known to all of us, by certain signs of a ship and of a sword belt."

"Then she must obey the custom of the castle."

"I am weary of the customs of castles," said Galahad. "What is this one?"

"It is that every maiden of noble birth to pass this way must pay passage dues, not in gold, but in blood from her right arm."

"That is an ugly custom," said Galahad.

And Percival moved closer to his sister.

"It is still the custom," said the leader, urging his horse closer. "The dues must be paid."

"Not while the strength is in my sword arm," said Galahad.

"Or in mine," said Percival.

"Or yet in mine," said Bors.

And as the knights came thrusting about them, they drew their swords and turned shoulder to shoulder, facing outwards all ways, with the maiden Anchoret in their midst. And when the knights charged in on them, they hurled them back. But scarcely was the fighting begun, when a score more knights came riding out from the castle and ringed them round. Then the attackers drew back a little, panting. "You are three valiant fighting-men," said the leader, "and so we have no wish to kill you. But even you cannot burst out of this circle; and as to the maiden, it will be all one in the end. Yield her up now, and go free."

"Such freedom would not taste over-sweet," said Galahad.

"Then you are bent on dying?"

"As God wills. But it is not yet come to that." Galahad brought up his sword.

Then the fighting burst out again, fierce and furious; and the knights drove in upon the three companions from all sides. All day they fought, until the shadows grew long and were lost in dusk, and the dusk deepened into the dark and they could no longer see the sword strokes. Then a trumpet sounded from the castle to break off the fray. And as the three stood leaning on their weary swords, the horsemen still ringed around them, more men came from the castle, bearing torches, and behind the torch-bearers an old white-haired man with a gold chain about his neck, who said to the companions, "Sirs, the last of the fighting-light is gone from the sky. Therefore it is time to call a truce. Do you come back now with us to the castle, and have safe lodging for the night. No harm shall come to you nor to the maiden while darkness lasts, and in the morning you shall all return to this place and state in which you stand now, and the fighting shall go forward as though there had been no pause between one sword-stroke and the next."

And the maiden Anchoret said, "Let us go with them. We shall be safe under the truce; and I know in my heart that this is the thing we are to do."

So they went with the old man and the castle knights, through the deep gateway into the stronghold. And there they were made welcome as honoured guests. And when supper was over in the Great Hall, the old man told them more concerning the custom of the castle.

"Some two years ago, the lady of this place, whose knights we are, fell sick of that dread disease, leprosy. We sent for every physician far and near, but none could heal her sickness. At last, a wise man told us that if she were bathed with the blood of a maiden, who was of noble birth, and who had never sinned in fact or in thought, our mistress would be instantly healed. Therefore no high-born maiden passes this way, that we do not take from her a bowlful of her blood. That is all the story."

"And yet the blood of these maidens has not healed your lady," said Sir Bors.

"Alas, no. It must be that none to pass this way so far has been altogether without sin."

When the telling was done, the maiden Anchoret called her three companions to her, and said, "Sirs, you have heard how it is with this lady, and that it lies in my power to give her healing. Now I know for what purpose the ship has brought us to this morning's harbour."

"If you do this thing," said Galahad, "I think that you will lose your life to save hers."

"That I know," said Anchoret. "But I know also, as I have known from the moment that I was told to cut my hair, what pathway I follow. Therefore let the three of you, who are most dear to me, give me your leave, for I would sooner do this with your leave and your blessing than without."

Then the three bowed their heads and gave her the leave that she asked for.

And she called to all those in the hall, "Be happy! For tomorrow your lady shall be well again!"

Next morning, they heard Mass together, and then returned to the Great Hall. And the people of the castle brought their lady from the chamber where she lay. And as she came, horror rose in Bors and Percival, and despite themselves they gave back a little at sight of her terrible leper's face when she put back her veil. Only Sir Galahad stood his ground, and bowed to her gravely in all courtesy; and the maiden Anchoret moved forward.

"You are come to heal me?" said the lady, as well as she could through her crumbling lips.

"Lady, I come, and I am ready. Let them bring the bowl."

Then the same maiden who had followed the knights out from the castle yesterday came carrying the same silver bowl. And standing before them all as straight and sweet as a young poplar tree, Anchoret held out her arm over it, and the old man brought a little bright knife, and opened one of the veins that showed blue under her fair skin, like the branching veins on an iris petal.

The red blood sprang out, and swiftly the bowl began to fill.

When it was almost brimming, Anchoret began to sway on her feet, as though a cold wind were in the slender branches of the poplar tree. She turned her face to the lady, and said, "Madam, to give you healing, I am come to my death. Pray for my soul."

And with the words scarce spoken, she fell back fainting into the arms of the three companions who sprang forward to catch her.

They laid her down, and did all that might be done to staunch the bleeding, but it had gone too far with her.

She opened her eyes after a while, but they all knew that she was dying; and when she spoke to Percival, her voice had grown so faint and far away that he had to bend close to catch her words.

"Dear brother, I beg you not to leave my body buried in this country. But as soon as my life is gone, carry me back to the ship, and let me go where fate and the wind shall bear me. I promise you this, that whenever you reach the holy city of Sarras, where the Grail Quest will assuredly take you in the end, you will find me there. And in that city, and nowhere else, pray you make my grave."

Weeping, Percival promised her.

She spoke once more, "Tomorrow, part from each other and go your separate ways, until your paths shall bring you together again to the Grail Castle of Corbenic. This, through me, is Our Lord's command to you."

And she gave the quietest of sighs, and the life went out from her.

And within the hour, when she had been bathed with the blood of the maiden, the lady of the castle was whole and well again, her blackened and hideous flesh restored to all its bloom; and she was young and beautiful once more, to the great rejoicing of all her people.

But Galahad and Percival and Bors set about their own tasks in sorrow. And when she had been made ready and all things fitly done, they carried the maiden's body on a litter spread with softest silks, back to the ship waiting in the harbour, and laid her there amidships. And Percival her brother set between her folded hands a letter he had written, telling who she was and how she had come to die, and setting forth on fair parchment the events of the Grail Quest in which she had taken part, that anyone who found her body on foreign shores might treat it with the more honour, knowing all her story.

Then they pushed the vessel off from the shore, and watched her drift quietly out to sea. For as long as they could still see the ship, they waited on the water's side; and when she was quite gone, they turned back to the castle.

The lady and her knights would have had them enter and rest, but they would not set foot in the place again, but asked that their arms should be brought out to them. So the people of the castle brought out their harness and weapons, and for each of them a horse, and they armed themselves and mounted, and set forth on their way once more.

But they had not gone far when great storm clouds began to gather, and it grew dark as late evening, though it was scarce past noon. And seeing a chapel beside the track, they stabled their horses in a rough shelter outside, and went in. Hardly had they done so, when the bulging black bellies of the storm clouds burst into thunder and lightning and lashing rain. And looking back from their shelter, the way that they had come, they saw the whole sky split open above the castle, and flaming thunderbolts hurtling down upon it. And above the roar of the tempest, they could hear the crash of falling towers.

All night the storm raged, but towards dawn the thunder ceased and the clouds parted and drifted away, and the sky grew clear and gentle, washed with light from the sun that was not yet risen.

Then the three companions rode back to see what had become of the castle. When they came to the gatehouse, it was scorched and ruined; and riding inside they found nothing but fallen stones and the bodies of men and women lying where the tempest of God's wrath had struck them down.

The lady of the castle had not kept her restored health and beauty long.

"The ways of the Grail Quest are indeed strange past men's understanding," said Percival, thinking of his sister.

They dismounted and hitched their horses to some fallen roof timbers in the courtyard, and went looking from place to place to see if any living thing yet survived. And so they came at last to the castle chapel, and behind it a small enclosed burial ground, with soft green grass, and late-flowering white roses arching their thorny sprays over the gravestones, a pleasant and peaceful place, and the storm had passed it by untouched. And as they moved among the stones, reading the names on each, they knew that it was the resting place of all the other maidens who had died for the sake of the lady.

After a while, they turned away and went back to their horses, and rode together until the moor was passed and the dark trees of the forest came to meet them. And there they checked, and took their leave of each other, as the maiden Anchoret had bidden them. "God keep you," they said, "God bring us all to our meeting place again at Corbenic Castle."

And they rode their three separate ways into the forest.

But now the story leaves Sir Galahad and Sir Percival and Sir Bors and tells again of Sir Lancelot, with his horse slain, lying beside the great river.

I 2

SIR LANCELOT
COMES TO CORBENIC

Now as Sir Lancelot lay in the shelter of his rock on the
river bank, between sleeping and waking, he heard a
voice in his inmost depths that said, "Lancelot, rise
now, and take your armour, and go on board the ship
that is waiting for you."

And when, startled, he opened his eyes, he found
himself lying in a pool of brilliant silver light, so that he

looked to the sky, thinking that the moon must have risen. But there was no moon. Then, with the words still echoing in the hollows of his head like the sea echoing in a shell, he got up and armed himself. And all the while the strange radiance was still about him, growing and spreading down to the margin of the river, showing him at last a ship lying there at rest like a great white sea bird among the reeds.

He went down the bank towards it. And as he went, the light faded, till the night was like any other. Only the blur of the ship still showed moth-pale through the reeds and alders.

He stepped aboard; and as he did so, it seemed to him that the air was full of fragrance—the scent as of all the spices in the world that had flooded through Arthur's Great Hall at Pentecost; of other things too, that were hard to give a name to, such as May mornings and applewood fires and well-oiled harness leather when he was a boy and his first honour hard and clean within him. And for one moment he was near to weeping, and in the next, joy leapt up in him like a cage-freed bird. And he prayed, "Lord, Lord, Lord, I have done as you bade me; I am in your hands, do with me as you will."

And as the wind woke in the sail, and the vessel slipped downriver towards the sea, he settled himself down against the side of the ship and drifted into a sleep that was itself like a blessing.

When he woke, it was morning, and the ship was far out of sight of any land. And looking about him, he saw, behind the single mast, a low couch or litter draped in silk; and on the couch, a maiden lying as though in quiet sleep. He drew near, softly, so as not to disturb her; but when he came beside the couch, he saw that she was dead. And he saw also the letter which Percival had set between her hands. Very gently, he took and unfolded it; and read all that was written; how she was Percival's sister, and how he and Bors and Galahad had placed her there, and of all the happenings of the Grail Quest that had gone before. Then he gave the maiden back her letter, and knelt down beside her to make his morning prayer.

And the gladness was in him, that the three so far ahead of him in the Quest had been together in that ship, and the maiden with them; and that they had, as it seemed, left word for him and reached back to draw him into their company.

So for a month and more Sir Lancelot was in the ship, and the winds and tides took him where they chose. And in all that time he was never hungry, though there were no stores on board; for every morning when he had done praying, it seemed that he had been fed with all that he could need until the next morning came. And he was never lonely, for in some strange way the dead maiden kept him gentle company, as she lay unchanging like one that slept. And it seemed that they shared together the autumn storms, and the stars of quiet nights, and the singing of the seas.

And then one night the ship came to shore again, where a dark forest marched down almost to the margin of the sea. And as he waited, not sure for what, but sure that he waited for something, Lancelot heard sounds that he knew must mean a horseman coming through the forest; the soft beat of hooves on leaf mould, and a great brushing aside of low-hanging branches.

Nearer drew the sounds, and nearer yet; and out on to the open shore rode a knight, who checked at sight of the waiting ship; then dismounted and, unsaddling his horse, turned it loose to wander where it would, and came on across the shore-grass and the shingle without haste or hesitating, as though to a meeting long planned. Frosty moonlight burned on his shield as he came, and showed it white, blazoned with a cross so brilliant that even in that light, which steals all colour from the world, it blazed blood-red.

So Sir Lancelot saw again the knight with the red cross on his shield, who he had followed so long and so desperately at the outset of the Quest.

His hand moved towards his sword, but did not draw it from its sheath, for it seemed that to do so might in some way disturb the maiden. And as the newcomer climbed aboard, he said, "Sir knight, I give you welcome."

The knight checked, and looked towards him in the shadow of the sail. "God's greeting to you. Pray you tell me who you are?"

"I am called Lancelot of the Lake," said Sir Lancelot. "Now do me the like courtesy and tell me by what name you are called."

For answer, the other unlaced and pulled off his helm. And as the white moonlight fell upon his face, Sir Lancelot stepped out from the shadow of the sail; and they stood and looked at each other as they had done in the abbey guest chamber on Pentecost Eve.

And the young knight saw the strange crooked face with one brow level as a falcon's wing and one flying wild like a mongrel's ear, but all worn down to bone and spirit since he saw it last. And the old knight saw the boy's face that had become a man's; a face that was gravely beautiful, but yet without a soft line in it anywhere, and a look of inner certainty that he had never seen in any man's face before. And from both faces, the same eyes looked out at each other.

Then Lancelot said, "Galahad! So it was you!"

And Galahad, who seldom smiled, smiled ruefully and said, "Forgive me. It was I, my father."

And they put their arms round each other and strained close. And for a while neither spoke again, for they could not find the words to say.

And then they fell to talking both at once. And all through what remained of that night they crouched in the bows of the ship, each telling the other of all that had befallen them since they set out on the Quest. And Galahad told his father of Bors and Percival and the maiden Anchoret, all those things for which there had been no room in the letter between her hands. And while they were still talking, the sun rose up, and it was another day.

For all the winter half of that year it was given to Lancelot and Galahad his son to be together in the ship, since it was the only time that ever they were to share in this life. And many times the ship put in to islands and unknown shores far from the world of men. And many were the strange and wonderful adventures that they met with when they went ashore together. But the story does not tell of these, for it would take too long in the telling, and draw no nearer to the mystery of the Grail. But always they returned to the ship, and the maiden lying there as though asleep. And there were times when Galahad left his body behind for good manners' sake, while he went away into the solitude and the desert places within himself. But now Lancelot had learned enough to let him go; and so the bond between them grew very strong.

And then the year turned to spring, and Easter was come and gone; and the leaf buds were breaking on the bare forest trees that rang with bird-song, when the ship came yet another time to land. And as they touched shore, a knight came out of the woods, riding a tall warhorse and leading in his right hand another as white as the wild pear blossom of the woodshore.

Seeing them where they waited on the deck of the ship, he came on at a hand-canter, and reining in, spoke to Galahad. "Sir knight, you have been as long as it is permitted you with your father. Now leave this ship, and mount and ride, for the Quest is waiting."

Then Galahad put his arm round his father's shoulders, as though he were the stronger and older of the two, and said, "I knew that, soon or late, this was how it must be; and my heart is sore within me, for I do not think that we shall meet again in this world."

And then he went ashore. And Sir Lancelot, still standing on the deck as though he were rooted there, with the grief in him darkening the spring day, said, "Pray for me, that I may keep faith with the Lord God both in this world and the next."

And Sir Galahad said, "I will pray, because you are my father, and there is love between us, and you ask it. But your own prayers are strong, and by your own prayers you shall surely keep faith."

And he mounted and rode away into the forest towards the cuckoo's calling, while the messenger who had come for him rode another way.

And as Sir Lancelot stood there looking after him, a rushing wind filled the sails and bore the vessel swiftly from the shore. So he was alone again, save for the body of the maiden Anchoret.

Then, kneeling beside her, Sir Lancelot prayed as even he had never prayed before, more humbly and more fiercely and with more of urgent longing, that if he was not indeed outcast from God's love, he might be allowed one more sight of the Grail, and that he might see it, not as he had done that other time beside the wayside cross, but with his heart and soul quick and answering within him.

Long and long he prayed, through nights and days, scarcely leaving off even to sleep. And then one night, when he ceased for a little from his praying, he found that he was no longer at sea, but far up the shrunken remains of what must once have been a broad river, and the ship had drifted into the deep inlet that yet remained, among rocks below a great castle.

And looking, he saw that he was below the rear towers of Corbenic.

Corbenic where he had come in his youth to the Lady Elaine, and where Galahad his son had been born. He knew it well, even after twenty years. And yet it was not Corbenic as he remembered it, but in some way strange; and looking far up the rock-cut steps that led from the shore to the river gate, he saw that the gate stood wide, and that it was guarded—the moon was very bright— by two lions standing face to face before the threshold.

And as he hesitated, wondering what he should do, a voice out of the moonlight said, "Lancelot, for you also it is time to leave the ship. Go up into the castle, for it is the place of your heart's desire."

So Lancelot hastily armed himself, leaving nothing behind that he had brought on board with him, and looked once in leave-taking towards the body of the maiden Anchoret, and scrambled ashore. And as he climbed up the rock stairway, the ship drifted out into mid-river and down towards the sea again.

At the head of the stairway the lions stood waiting, and Lancelot set his hand ready to the hilt of his sword. But before he had need to draw it, they pulled back from the gateway and sat down on their haunches like hounds. And so he passed through between them into the town, and went on up the steep main street until he came to the fortress itself. It was midnight, and the moon shone down, and all the people of the town and the castle were abed, and no guards anywhere, and all the gates standing open as though they waited for his coming. And his mailed feet rang hollow on the stones of the vaulted stair that led up to the Great Hall, but none came to see who walked that way.

So he went on, following his own shadow on the moonlit floors, until he came to a part of the castle that he did not know at all, and a stairway leading up once more.

Again he climbed. And at the head of the stair he came to a closed door, the first closed door that had met him in all that while. He pushed against it, but it did not open to him.

He tried again and again, but there was no latch to the door, and for all his pushing it yielded no more than if it had been part of the solid wall.

And as he stood there, desperately wondering what to do next, for he was sure that he must open that door if he was to come to the thing he sought, a strain of music reached him from beyond the unyielding timbers. It was music sweeter than any singing of this world, and braided into the shining cadences he seemed to catch the words, "Glory and praise and honour be thine, Father of Heaven." And then he thought that his heart must surely burst, for he knew the Grail was within the chamber beyond that door, and he was once again shut out.

He knelt down, close against the door timbers, and prayed with his head bowed into his cupped hands, "Dear God, my sins are heavy on me. But if ever I did anything that pleased you, of your pity, do not bar me altogether from that which I have sought so long."

He thought he heard a faint sound of something moving, and the music swelled louder on his ear. And when he looked up from between his hands, he was dazzled as though he were looking into the sun. The door stood wide, and the chamber beyond it blazed like a golden rose in the heart of the dark castle. Light flooded out from it, and a beauty that was more than the flowers and the candles and the singing, that pierced him through and licked him round and drew him so that he stumbled to his feet and was half into the chamber when the voice spoke to him again.

"Back, Sir Lancelot. It is given to you to see, but not to enter in."

So Sir Lancelot drew back from the place of his heart's desire, and knelt humbly on the threshold, looking in.

Afterwards he was never sure whether he had actually seen the flowers and the candles and heard the music, any more than he was sure whether he had actually seen the chamber full of the rainbowed sweep of angels' wings. But he knew that, as he knelt there, he saw again at the very heart of the blaze and the beauty the Holy Grail, under its veil of samite.

And kneeling before the Grail there was an aged priest. Perhaps it was Josephus himself, perhaps not; there seemed no time in that place, no barrier between those living in this world and those living in Heaven; and anyway, he was beyond thinking. Only he knew that the priest was celebrating the Mass, and that at the crowning moment when he rose and turned holding aloft the cup, there were three others in the chamber; and for an instant he thought that they must be Bors and Percival and Galahad; and then he knew that they were not, though he could not see them for their brightness. And two of them were placing the Third in the up-stretched hands of the priest. And then Sir Lancelot was not sure whether the priest held up the Third, or whether he was the Third himself, and it was something else he carried; something much too heavy for him, so that it bowed him almost to the ground.

Then Lancelot forgot that he was forbidden to enter the chamber, and knew only that he must help—must take some of the weight. And he got up and stumbled across the threshold with his hands held out.

He was met by a puff of wind laced with flame that scorched and blinded him. Darkness rushed in upon him from all sides; and he felt hands, many hands, that flung him backwards out of the chamber, so that he fell all asprawl across the stairhead; and the darkness engulfed him where he lay.

13

THE LOOSING
OF THE WATERS

Next day when the castle awoke and people were once
more stirring all about, they found Sir Lancelot lying as
though stunned by a heavy blow outside the door of the
Grail chamber. They knew who he was, for many of the
older knights remembered him well across the twenty
years between; but how he came to be where he was,
and in his present state, they did not know, save that he
must have been seeking the Grail.

They carried him to a turret chamber far from the
noise and bustle of the great castle, and laid him on the

bed and, unarming him, searched him all over for wounds, but found no mark upon him save for the silvery traces of old hurts, for he was scarred like an old and well-tried hunting dog.

So they laid the covers over him and let him lie, until he should come to himself, seeing that there was nothing more they could do for him but let him rest. But the days went by and the nights went by, while always somebody sat watching him by sunlight or rainlight or the light of a silver lamp; and Sir Lancelot never moved nor spoke. And here and there a lady in the Great Chamber who remembered him when she was a maiden, or the youngest scullion in the kitchens who had never seen him at all but heard stories told by the old kennelman who had, wept a little to think of the greatest knight in the world brought so low.

Twenty-four days, and twenty-four nights. And then around noon on the twenty-fifth day, Sir Lancelot opened his eyes and looked about him with an eager light in his face, as though he still thought to see what he had seen in the Grail chamber. Then the light faded, as he knew and accepted his loss.

He looked at those about his bed and asked, "How is it that I come to be in this chamber? How long have I lain here?"

And they told him what they knew of his coming, and how long he had lain there like one dead.

Then Sir Lancelot said that he must ride; and after food had been fetched to give him strength, and he had eaten, a maiden brought him a fair new linen tunic. But he saw the cruel hair shirt that he had worn for more than half a year lying on a chest beside the bed, and took that up instead.

An old and gentle knight among those gathered about him said, "There are those among us who know what cannot be spoken in words. There is no more need that you wear that now. For you, the Quest of the Grail is over; and you have travelled as far as you may along that road."

Sir Lancelot looked at him, and smiled; a shadow of his old lopsided smile. "That I know. For me, now, there is only the way back. Yet I did not take this shirt of penitence only for so long as I followed the Quest, but if it may be so, for all of life that remains to me." And he pulled on the horsehair garment next his skin, and then the fine linen over it lest the maiden who had brought it should be hurt; and over that a gown of crimson wool that had also been brought for him.

Four days more he remained at Corbenic, gathering back his strength; and on the fifth he asked for his armour to be brought to him, for he wished to return to Arthur's kingdom, from which he had been absent more than a year.

So a squire fetched his harness and weapons and helped him to arm; and when he went down to the castle courtyard, he found a swift and fiery chestnut horse being walked up and down there.

"It is a gift from King Pelles," they said, "from the Grail Keeper, the Maimed King."

"Pray you give him my thanks," Sir Lancelot said, "and may God be with him."

And he mounted, and leaving the Grail Castle behind him, rode on his way.

Yet he did not at once return to King Arthur's court. He knew that for him the Quest was spent and over; yet now there was an unwillingness in him to turn round and ride home; a dread of what he would find there; the empty places at the Round Table; a dread, maybe, of seeing Queen Guenever again. After all the stress and struggle, he needed a threshold time before returning to the world once more.

Also there was a feeling in him of something still to happen, still to be waited for. And so, while all that summer and autumn and winter went by, he rode errant in the Waste Land, giving himself to any adventure that came his way; and waiting, always waiting, he did not know for what, until spring came round again, the poor shabby spring of the Waste Forest.

Once he heard from a charcoal burner that Galahad and Bors and Percival had been seen riding together again; and then he knew that the fulfilment of the Quest must be near for them, and he was glad. But he did not go seeking them, for he knew that his path did not lead that way.

One night, being far from any village or hermitage or forester's hut, he lay down supperless to sleep under a half-dead willow tree by the last trickle of an all but dried-out stream, choosing the place because there was a little sparse grass there for his horse to graze.

And sleeping there with his shield for a pillow, he dreamed.

He dreamed that he was back on the threshold of the Grail chamber at Corbenic, seeing it all as it had been before. But now Galahad and Percival and Bors were there; and there also, lying on a couch, was King Pelles himself. The light and the singing and the beauty made a bright cloud in Lancelot's head, so that he could not see to the heart of the glory. But, as before, he knew that the Mass was going forward, and he saw the Grail, and beside it a spear whose blade dripped red. And he knew, though he heard no voice, that they were receiving their orders, to take the Grail back to the holy city of Sarras, from which it had come so long ago, that from there it might return to its true place. There was another order, too, for Galahad alone; and he saw Galahad take up the spear and carry it to the Maimed King, and touch the gaping wound on his thigh with the blood that dripped from the blade. And he saw King Pelles rise whole and strong once more from the couch on which he lay. And then he seemed to catch the voice at last; or maybe it was another voice; and it said, "Now the waters are loosed and the rivers shall run, and the Waste Land shall put forth wheat and the cattle bear many young, and the birds shall sing in the trees among the broad leaves of summer."

And then he woke; and the glory became the first sunlight slanting into his eyes, and the birds were singing as he had never heard them sing in the Waste Forest before, as though they were singing for the first morning of the world. And then another sound came to his ears; the swift purl of running water; and as he raised himself on his arm and looked about him, he saw, clear through the green mist of buds that seemed breaking on the willow branches even while he looked, that the stream below him, that had been no more than a chain of stagnant puddles, was running swift and deep. And his great warhorse went brushing down through the willow branches to drink.

And he knew that he had dreamed true; and the Maimed King was whole again, and his land whole again with him; and the Grail was away to its own place, and Galahad and his companions with it.

The waiting was over; and when he had whistled up his horse and saddled it, he mounted and turned its head towards Camelot.

And now, for the last time, the story leaves Sir Lancelot, and tells of Sir Galahad and Sir Bors and Sir Percival.

14

THE GRAIL

Now for Sir Galahad and Sir Bors and Sir Percival, all
had been just as Sir Lancelot had seen it in his dream.
But they had seen and heard and known all that for him
had been mercifully hidden in the brightness of the
glory. And their souls were raised up and sat loose
within them as a sword half-drawn from its sheath.

And obeying the voice, they armed themselves and
went down to the seashore out beyond the mouth of the
great river.

And there they found the proud ship which had given
Galahad his sword. And looking down into her, they
saw under the canopy the bed with the golden crown
still lying at its head. But at the foot, where Galahad had

left his old sword lying in place of the other, stood the silver table which they had last seen in the Grail chamber of the castle far behind them; and on the table, the Grail itself, under a veil of crimson samite.

"Brothers," said Galahad, "this is the last of our journeys. May God go with us." And they stepped on board.

And at once the great wind that they knew so well woke in the far corners of the sky and came sweeping into the sail, and drove the ship out from land and sent her skimming over the waves.

For many days they journeyed so; and their bodies were never hungry while the Grail was with them. And at last, without their having glimpsed any land between, the wind fell from their sails, and the ship came drifting into the harbour of a great city; and they knew by its beauty and by the light that shone about it, that it must be Sarras, the Sacred City, which is, as it were, the threshold of the City of God.

And as they drew alongside the quay, they heard the voice again. "Now leave the ship, and take up the silver table with its burden, and carry it up into the city, not once setting it down until you come to the church which is the city's crown. Then set down the Grail in its old lodging place."

So they took up the silver table between them, and stepped ashore. And as they did so, a second vessel came gliding into the harbour, and looking towards it, they saw the white samite sails shining in the morning sun, and the body of the maiden Anchoret lying amidships where they had laid her so many months before.

"Truly," said Galahad, "the maiden has kept her promise well."

Then, with Bors and Percival in front and Galahad at the rear, they set to carrying the silver table with the Grail upon it, through steep streets between honeycomb golden houses up into the Sacred City. But with every step they took, the weight of the silver table and its burden grew greater and greater, until, by the time they drew towards the gate of the Sacred City they were near to exhaustion.

Now in the arched gateway sat a crippled beggar, all bent and twisted together, with his crutch and his begging bowl beside him. And seeing him there, Galahad called out to him, "Friend, come and take the fourth corner of this table and help us on our way."

"Alas," said the man, "gladly would I help you, but you see how it is with me. It is ten years since I walked unaided."

"You see how it is with us," returned Galahad, "that we are forespent under the weight of that which we bear. Do not be afraid. Get up, now, and try."

And the beggar's eyes were fixed on the Grail under its samite covering. And it seemed to all those watching that under the samite there began to be a glow that was not the sunlight, for the narrow street was deep in shade. And he made a little whimpering sound and got up, slowly and unsteadily, but as straight as ever he had been. And the strength rushed into him, and he came gladly and took the fourth corner of the silver table. And suddenly it seemed that there was no weight to it at all.

So they went through the gate and up into the Sacred City, with a great rejoicing crowd gathering to them, more and more at every step, as word went ringing round Sarras of what it was they carried, and of the healing of the beggar man. And when they came to the great church that was the living heart of the city, they set the Grail down before the high altar. Then they went back to the harbour again, where the second ship waited for them.

There, too, a crowd was gathered, looking on in awe and wonder; and Galahad and his two companions went on board and lifted the litter on which the maiden lay, and carried her up through the steep, thronged streets, to the church in the Sacred City where the priests were by now gathered, and set her down beside the Grail. And the light, shining in through the high windows of stained glass, splashed her white robes with the colours of rose and foxglove and iris and all the fairest flowers of summer.

And there before the altar she was buried, with such ceremonies as befitted a king's daughter.

But when word of all this was brought to the King of the city, Escorant by name, he sent for them and demanded the meaning of what he heard. And they answered truthfully every question that he asked; and told him the whole story of the Grail Quest. But the eyes of his spirit were blind, and he believed no word of all they said, but called them vile impostors, and summoning his guards, had them thrown into prison.

"And let you lie there and rot," said he, "until you bethink you of a better story."

For a year, they remained in their prison, but as it had been with Joseph and his people when they were held captive in Britain, the Lord God sent the Holy Grail to comfort and keep them all the time of their captivity.

And at the end of a year, King Escorant lay sick, and knew that he was near to dying. And he thought of the three captives in his dungeons, and his heart was changed within him, so that he sent for Galahad and Percival and Bors. And when they stood before him in their prison filth, he begged their forgiveness for his evil treatment of them.

And they forgave him fully and freely, even Bors, who found forgiveness harder than the other two. And in that same hour, he died.

Now King Escorant left no son to follow him; and so when he had been laid in his splendid tomb, the people of Sarras began to wonder among themselves who they should have for their next king. And their choice turned toward Sir Galahad, remembering how he and his companions had come bringing back the Grail, and of his healing of the lame beggar at the Sacred City gate. And they said, "Surely we could choose no better king than this one."

When their chief men came and told Galahad this, he said, "That was none of my doing, but the power of the Grail."

And the chief men said, "Even though that be so, there is another reason. King Escorant had no blood-right to the crown; but you are of the line of Joseph of Arimathea, and you have brought back to this city the Grail which he brought here long ago. Therefore it is fitting to the end of this mighty and mysterious adventure that you should bear the golden weight of the crown, even if it be for a single day."

So Galahad was crowned King of Sarras, though indeed he had no wish for it and the goldwork seemed as sharp as thorns upon his forehead.

On the morning after the crowning, Galahad rose in the first paling of the dawn, and put on his well-worn harness that he had carried through so many adventures. Only he left aside his helm, and let his mail coif lie unlaced on his shoulders so that his head was bare. And he called Bors and Percival to him, and together they went up from the palace to the church in the midst of the Sacred City.

When they came into the tall-towered church, where the colour was newly waking in the eastern windows, they looked towards the high altar and the Grail in its usual place. And standing there, they saw one in the vestments of a bishop. It seemed to them that he was the same priest whom they had seen in the Grail chamber at Corbenic. And indeed it seemed that he knew them also; for as soon as they had crossed the threshold, he spoke to them in greeting. And to Sir Galahad, who was now King of Sarras, he said, "Galahad, come now, and see and share in this that you have so longed for."

And Galahad drew near, the others moving a little behind him, and, kneeling, looked into the Cup which the priest had uncovered and held out to him.

Behind him, Bors and Percival saw nothing but the strangely wrought golden vessel. They had shared in the mystery at Corbenic, and this time it was not for them, only the awe and the joy and the reverence that they had always known at Mass. This was the last mystery that Galahad must go to alone, no matter how close they knelt behind him, as each man goes alone to his birth and his dying.

They saw his whole body begin to shake, as though a great wind were blowing through him. He looked up; and his face, with the first sunlight of the morning upon it, shone as though it were lit from within; and his eyes were full of all that the others could not see.

He held up his hands and cried out in a great glad voice, "Lord, I give thee thanks, that thou hast granted me my soul's desire. Here is the wonder that passes every wonder, that heart cannot conceive nor tongue relate. Now grant me that I come to you!"

And he fell headlong, the clash of his armour on the marble pavement ringing through the empty spaces under the high arched roof. For he had seen into the heart of all things, where no man may look and continue living in his body.

Bors and Percival sprang to gather him in their arms, and he looked from one to the other in farewell. To Bors, he said, "When you come to Camelot again, greet Sir Lancelot, my lord father, for me, and take to him my love."

And his head fell back against Percival's shoulder.

And suddenly, to the two left behind, it seemed that the emptiness of the great church was full of the sweep of wings and the glory of unheard music; and Heaven itself opened, and a hand came down and took the Grail from before the altar, and returned whence it came.

And Heaven closed in their faces, leaving only the emptiness of the great church behind. Even the man in bishop's robes was gone; and they were alone, and Galahad was dead.

And grief took them such as no grief they had ever known before.

The people of Sarras, too, mourned for Sir Galahad. They made him a grave where he had died, close beside the spot where the maiden Anchoret lay; and buried him with all the honours due to a king.

And when that was done, Sir Percival laid aside his

old knightly dress, and put on the rough habit of a hermit, and with Bors's help made himself a wattle cabin outside the city walls in which to spend the rest of his life in prayer and contemplation.

Sir Bors stayed with him in faithful friendship; but he never laid aside his sword nor changed his harness for a hermit's garb, for he knew that when Percival had no more need of him, the lines of his own life would lead him back to Britain and King Arthur's court. And he knew, to his sorrow, that the time would not be long. From the first moment of their first meeting, Percival had followed Galahad, and he would follow him still.

Percival lived just one year and three days after Sir Galahad, and then was laid beside his friend and his sister, in the church at the heart of the Sacred City of Sarras.

Then Sir Bors, being alone, put on his armour, and went down to the harbour and boarded a ship sailing westward. And after many days at sea, he came to his own shores at last, and took horse for Camelot.

When he arrived there was great rejoicing, for it was full two years since Sir Lancelot had returned, and he had been the last, until now, of the Grail knights to come home; so that the King and his court had long ago given up Sir Bors as lost to them, along with Sir Galahad and Sir Percival.

He found his brother Lional there, and Sir Gawain with a scar on his head, and Sir Ector of the Marsh, and other old friends. But many more were lacking; and when they sat down to eat that evening, half the places at the Round Table were empty, and among those missing were many of the best who used to sit there. And of those who were there, many had wounds and scars, and most were changed in some way from what they had been before. And he thought that the high adventure of the Grail had been a costly one. He knew that the end had been victory, but he was too weary to see how.

When the evening meal was over, he sought out Sir Lancelot his kinsman. He had noticed that the older knight ate no meat and drank no wine at supper; and he thought that at the neck of his fine silken tunic he had glimpsed the rough edge of a hair shirt, and the redness of chafed skin beneath. He took him aside, up to the rampart above the castle garden, where it was possible to speak and be sure that no one else was by to hear. "Sir," he said, "I bring you a message. Galahad got his soul's desire, and died in my arms and Percival's, for he had come into the heart of the mystery, where it is not possible for a mortal man to come, and yet remain mortal. And with his last breath he bade me greet you from him, and bring you his love."

"I wish I could have been with him," said Sir Lancelot, heavily.

"So did he. So did we all. Often we spoke of you, and wished that you might be among us."

"There was a reason why that could not be," said Sir Lancelot, "A reason—a holding back . . . It was not all mine to give . . . Not for me alone, to renounce, you see . . ."

His voice had grown absent and inward-turning, as though he spoke to himself within himself, and not to Bors at all. And Bors saw his eyes following something that moved below; and looking in the same direction, saw through the soft thickening light of the summer evening that the Queen had come into the garden.

Next day, when Bors was rested, the King sent for his clerks, who had taken down from each returning knight the story of his adventures on the Quest. And they took down Sir Bors's story, which was the only one that went beyond Sir Lancelot's and told of the last adventuring of Sir Galahad and Sir Percival and himself, and of the taking up to Heaven of the Grail.

And then the record was complete, and the King sent it for safe-keeping to the monks of the abbey library of Salisbury; that in future years the story of the Quest for the Holy Grail might not be lost to men coming after.